Granny's Tales

Ruskin Bond is known for his signature simplistic and witty writing style. He is the author of several bestselling short stories, novellas, collections, essays and children's books; and has contributed a number of poems and articles to various magazines and anthologies. At the age of twenty-three, he won the prestigious John Llewellyn Rhys Prize for his first novel, *The Room on the Roof.* He was also the recipient of the Padma Shri in 1999, Lifetime Achievement Award by the Delhi Government in 2012 and the Padma Bhushan in 2014.

Born in 1934, Ruskin Bond grew up in Jamnagar, Shimla, New Delhi and Dehradun. Apart from three years in the UK, he has spent all his life in India, and now lives in Landour, Mussoorie, with his adopted family.

RUSKIN BOND

Granny's Tales

RUPA

Published by
Rupa Publications India Pvt. Ltd 2022
7/16, Ansari Road, Daryaganj
New Delhi 110002

Sales centres:
Allahabad Bengaluru Chennai
Hyderabad Jaipur Kathmandu
Kolkata Mumbai

ISBN: 978-93-5520-765-4

First impression 2022

10 9 8 7 6 5 4 3 2 1

Moral right of the author has been asserted.

Printed in India

CONTENTS

INTRODUCTION

Some of our fondest memories that keep us company on a difficult day are ones from childhood. It is of the days we spent at our grandparents' house, running around with friends, reading under trees, complaining about how full our stomachs are and yet eyeing the candy that remind us of simpler times—uncomplicated and full of love.

Some of our favourite stories are the ones that our grandmothers told us. Sitting on kitchen counters, basking in the wonderful smells of granny's stew; lying on the bed mid-afternoon while Granny sews on a chair—these are the images that come to mind when we discern the formative memories of our life.

This book is an ode to such moments: Grandpa fighting an ostrich, bringing home monkeys of all shapes and sizes; Grandma ruling her home with an iron fist, yet having the most love and affection—just grandparents being our favourite, most sought-after caregivers. If there is a story worth telling, it is the ones that feature the people with the most capacity for love.

Ruskin Bond

THE CHERRY TREE

One day, when Rakesh was six, he walked home from the Mussoorie bazaar eating cherries. They were a little sweet, a little sour; small, bright red cherries which had come all the way from the Kashmir Valley.

Here in the Himalayan foothills where Rakesh lived, there were not many fruit trees. The soil was stony, and the dry cold winds stunted the growth of most plants. But on the more sheltered slopes there were forests of oak and deodar.

Rakesh lived with his grandfather on the outskirts of Mussoorie, just where the forest began. His father and mother lived in a small village fifty miles away, where they grew maize and rice and barley in narrow terraced fields on the lower slopes of the mountain. But there were no schools in the village, and Rakesh's parents were keen that he should go to school. As soon as he was of schoolgoing age, they sent him to stay with his grandfather in Mussoorie.

Grandfather was a retired forest ranger. He had a little cottage outside the town.

Rakesh was on his way home from school when he bought the cherries. He paid fifty paise for the bunch. It took him about half an hour to walk home, and by the time he reached the cottage there were only three cherries left.

'Have a cherry, Grandfather,' he said, as soon as he saw his grandfather in the garden.

Grandfather took one cherry and Rakesh promptly ate the other two. He kept the last seed in his mouth for some time, rolling it round and round on his tongue until all the tang had gone. Then he placed the seed on the palm of his hand and studied it.

'Are cherry seeds lucky?' asked Rakesh.

'Of course.'

'Then I'll keep it.'

'Nothing is lucky if you put it away. If you want luck, you must put it to some use.'

'What can I do with a seed?'

'Plant it.'

So Rakesh found a small spade and began to dig up a flower bed.

'Hey, not there,' said Grandfather. 'I've sown mustard in that bed. Plant it in that shady corner where it won't be disturbed.'

Rakesh went to a corner of the garden where the earth was soft and yielding. He did not have to dig. He pressed the seed into the soil with his thumb and it went right in.

Then he had his lunch and ran off to play cricket with his friends and forgot all about the cherry seed.

When it was winter in the hills, a cold wind blew down from the snows and went *whoo-whoo-whoo* through the deodar trees, and the garden was dry and bare. In the evenings, Grandfather told Rakesh stories—stories about people who turned into animals, and ghosts who lived in trees, and beans that jumped and stones that wept—and in turn Rakesh would read to him from the newspaper, Grandfather's eyesight being rather weak. Rakesh found the newspaper very dull—especially after the stories—but Grandfather wanted all the news...

They knew it was spring when the wild duck flew north again, to Siberia. Early in the morning, when he got up to chop wood and light a fire, Rakesh saw the V-shaped formation streaming northwards, the calls of the birds carrying clearly through the thin mountain air.

One morning in the garden, he bent to pick up what he thought was a small twig and found to his surprise that it was well-rooted. He stared at it for a moment, then ran to fetch Grandfather, calling, 'Dada, come and look, the cherry tree has come up!'

'What cherry tree?' asked Grandfather, who had forgotten about it.

'The seed we planted last year—look, it's come up!'

Rakesh went down on his haunches, while Grandfather bent almost double and peered down at the tiny tree. It was about four inches high.

'Yes, it's a cherry tree,' said Grandfather. 'You should water it now and then.'

Rakesh ran indoors and came back with a bucket of water.

'Don't drown it!' said Grandfather.

Rakesh gave it a sprinkling and circled it with pebbles.

'What are the pebbles for?' asked Grandfather.

'For privacy,' said Rakesh.

He looked at the tree every morning but it did not seem to be growing very fast. So he stopped looking at it—except quickly, out of the corner of his eye. And, after a week or two, when he allowed himself to look at it properly, he found that it had grown—at least an inch!

That year the monsoon rains came early and Rakesh plodded to and from school in a raincoat and gumboots. Ferns sprang from the trunks of trees, strange-looking lilies came up in the long grass, and even when it wasn't raining the trees dripped, and mist came curling up the valley. The cherry tree grew quickly in this season.

It was about two feet high when a goat entered the garden and ate all the leaves. Only the main stem and two thin branches remained.

'Never mind,' said Grandfather, seeing that Rakesh was upset. 'It will grow again, cherry trees are tough.'

Towards the end of the rainy season new leaves appeared on the tree. Then a woman cutting grass scrambled down the hillside, her scythe swishing through the heavy monsoon foliage. She did not try to avoid the tree: one sweep, and the cherry tree was cut in two.

When Grandfather saw what had happened, he went after the woman and scolded her; but the damage could not be repaired.

'Maybe it will die now,' said Rakesh.

'Maybe,' said Grandfather.

But the cherry tree had no intention of dying.

By the time summer came round again, it had sent out several new shoots with tender green leaves. Rakesh had grown taller too. He was eight now, a sturdy boy with curly black hair and deep black eyes. Blackberry eyes, Grandfather called them.

That monsoon Rakesh went home to his village, to help his father and mother with the planting and ploughing and sowing. He was thinner but stronger when he came back to Grandfather's house at the end of the rains, to find that the cherry tree had grown another foot. It was now up to his chest.

Even when there was rain, Rakesh would sometimes water the tree. He wanted it to know that he was there.

One day, he found a bright green praying mantis perched on a branch, peering at him with bulging eyes. Rakesh let it remain there. It was the cherry tree's first visitor.

The next visitor was a hairy caterpillar, who started making a meal of the leaves. Rakesh removed it quickly and dropped it on a heap of dry leaves.

'They're pretty leaves,' said Rakesh. 'And they are always ready to dance. If there's a breeze.'

After Grandfather had come indoors, Rakesh went into the garden and lay down on the grass beneath the tree. He gazed up through the leaves at the great blue sky; and turning on his side, he could see the mountain striding away into the clouds. He was still lying beneath the tree when the evening shadows crept across the garden. Grandfather came back and sat down beside Rakesh, and they waited in silence until the stars came out and the nightjar began to call. In the forest below, the crickets and cicadas began tuning up; and suddenly the tree was full of the sounds of insects.

'There are so many trees in the forest,' said Rakesh. 'What's so special about this tree? Why do we like it so much?'

'We planted it ourselves,' said Grandfather. 'That's why it's special.'

'Just one small seed,' said Rakesh, and he touched the smooth bark of the tree that had grown. He ran his hand along the trunk of the tree and put his finger to the tip of a leaf. 'I wonder,' he whispered, 'is this what it feels to be God?'

GRANDFATHER FIGHTS AN OSTRICH

Before my grandfather joined the Indian Railways, he worked for a few years on the East African Railways, and it was during that period that he had his now famous encounter with the ostrich. My childhood was frequently enlivened by this oft-told tale of his, and I give it here in his own words—or as well as I can remember them!

While engaged in the laying of a new railway line, I had a miraculous escape from an awful death. I lived in a small township, but my work lay some twelve miles away, and I had to go to the work-site and back on horseback.

One day, my horse had a slight accident, so I decided to do the journey on foot, being a great walker in those days. I also knew of a shortcut through the hills that would save me about six miles.

This shortcut went through an ostrich farm—or 'camp', as it was called. It was the breeding season. I was fairly familiar with the ways of ostriches, and knew that male birds were very aggressive in the breeding season, ready to attack on the slightest provocation, but I also knew that my dog would scare away any bird that might try to attack me. Strange though it may seem, even the biggest ostrich (and some of them grow to a height of nine feet) will run faster than a racehorse at the sight of even a small dog. So, I felt quite safe in the company of my dog, a mongrel who had adopted me some two months previously.

On arrival at the camp, I climbed through the wire fencing and, keeping a good look-out, dodged across the open spaces between the thorn bushes. Now and then I caught a glimpse of the birds feeding some distance away.

I had gone about half a mile from the fencing when up started a hare. In an instant my dog gave chase. I tried calling him back, even though I knew it was hopeless. Chasing hares was that dog's passion.

I don't know whether it was the dog's bark or my own shouting, but what I was most anxious to avoid immediately happened. The ostriches were startled and began darting to and fro. Suddenly, I saw a big male bird emerge from a thicket about a hundred yards away. He stood still and stared at me for a few moments. I stared back. Then, expanding his short wings and with his tail erect, he came bounding towards me.

As I had nothing, not even a stick, with which to defend myself, I turned and ran towards the fence. But it was an unequal race. What were my steps of two or three feet against the creature's great strides of sixteen to twenty feet? There was only one hope: to get behind a large bush and try to elude the bird until help came. A dodging game was my only chance.

And so, I rushed for the nearest clump of thorn bushes and waited for my pursuer. The great bird wasted no time—he was immediately upon me.

Then the strangest encounter took place. I dodged this way and that, taking great care not to get directly in front of the ostrich's deadly kick. Ostriches kick forward, and with such terrific force that if you were struck, their huge chisel-like nails would cause you much damage.

I was breathless, and really quite helpless, calling wildly for help as I circled the thorn bush. My strength was ebbing.

How much longer could I keep going? I was ready to drop from exhaustion.

As if aware of my condition, the infuriated bird suddenly doubled back on his course and charged straight at me. With a desperate effort, I managed to step to one side. I don't know how, but I found myself holding on to one of the creature's wings, quite close to its body.

It was now the ostrich's turn to be frightened. He began to turn, or rather waltz, moving round and round so quickly that my feet were soon swinging out from his body, almost horizontally! All the while, the ostrich kept opening and shutting his beak with loud snaps.

Imagine my situation as I clung desperately to the wing of the enraged bird. He was whirling me round and round as though he were a discus-thrower—and I the discus! My arms soon began to ache with the strain, and the swift and continuous circling was making me dizzy. But I knew that if I relaxed my hold, even for a second, a terrible fate awaited me.

Round and round we went in a great circle. It seemed as if that spiteful bird would never tire. And, I knew I could not hold on much longer. Suddenly, the ostrich went into reverse! This unexpected move made me lose my hold and sent me sprawling to the ground. I landed in a heap near the thorn bush and in an instant, before I even had time to realize what had happened, the big bird was upon me. I thought the end had come. Instinctively, I raised my hands to protect my face. But the ostrich did not strike.

I moved my hands from my face and there stood the creature with one foot raised, ready to deliver a deadly kick! I couldn't move. Was the bird going to play cat-and-mouse with me, and prolong the agony?

As I watched, frightened and fascinated, the ostrich turned

his head sharply to the left. A second later he jumped back, turned, and made off as fast as he could go. Dazed, I wondered what had happened to make him beat so unexpected a retreat.

I soon found out. To my great joy, I heard the bark of my truant dog, and the next moment he was jumping around me, licking my face and hands. Needless to say, I returned his caresses most affectionately! And, I took good care to see that he did not leave my side until we were well clear of that ostrich camp.

A TIGER IN THE HOUSE

Timothy, the tiger cub, was discovered by Grandfather on a hunting expedition in the Terai jungle near Dehra.

Grandfather was no shikari, but as he knew the forests of the Siwalik hills better than most people, he was persuaded to accompany the party—it consisted of several Very Important Persons from Delhi—to advise on the terrain and the direction the beaters should take once a tiger had been spotted.

The camp itself was sumptuous—seven large tents (one for each shikari), a dining tent and a number of servants' tents. The dinner was very good, as Grandfather admitted afterwards; it was not often that one saw hot-water plates, finger glasses and seven or eight courses in a tent in the jungle! But that was how things were done in the days of the viceroys… There were also some fifteen elephants, four of them with howdahs for the shikaris, and the others specially trained for taking part in the beat.

The sportsmen never saw a tiger, nor did they shoot anything else, though they saw a number of deer, peacock and wild boar. They were giving up all hope of finding a tiger and were beginning to shoot at jackals, when Grandfather, strolling down the forest path at some distance from the rest of the party, discovered a little tiger about eighteen inches long, hiding among the intricate roots of a banyan tree. Grandfather picked him up and brought him home after the camp had broken up. He had the distinction of being the only member of the party to have bagged any game, dead or alive.

At first the tiger cub, who was named Timothy by Grandmother, was brought up entirely on milk given to him in a feeding bottle by our cook, Mahmoud. But the milk proved too rich for him, and he was put on a diet of raw mutton and cod liver oil, to be followed later by a more tempting diet of pigeons and rabbits.

Timothy was provided with two companions—Toto the monkey, who was bold enough to pull the young tiger by the tail, and then climb up the curtains if Timothy lost his temper; and a small mongrel puppy, found on the road by Grandfather.

At first Timothy appeared to be quite afraid of the puppy and darted back with a spring if it came too near. He would make absurd dashes at it with his large forepaws and then retreat to a ridiculously safe distance. Finally, he allowed the puppy to crawl on his back and rest there!

One of Timothy's favourite amusements was to stalk anyone who would play with him, and so, when I came to live with Grandfather, I became one of the tiger's favourites. With a crafty look in his glittering eyes, and his body crouching, he would creep closer and closer to me, suddenly making a dash for my feet, rolling over on his back and kicking with delight, and pretending to bite my ankles.

He was by this time the size of a full-grown retriever, and when I took him out for walks, people on the road would give us a wide berth. When he pulled hard on his chain, I had difficulty in keeping up with him. His favourite place in the house was the drawing room, and he would make himself comfortable on the long sofa, reclining there with great dignity and snarling at anybody who tried to get him off.

Timothy had clean habits, and would scrub his face with

his paws exactly like a cat. At night, he slept in the cook's quarters and was always delighted at being let out by him in the morning.

'One of these days,' declared Grandmother in her prophetic manner, 'we are going to find Timothy sitting on Mahmoud's bed, and no sign of the cook except his clothes and shoes!'

Of course, it never came to that, but when Timothy was about six months old a change came over him; he grew steadily less friendly. When out for a walk with me, he would try to steal away to stalk a cat or someone's pet Pekingese. Sometimes at night we would hear frenzied cackling from the poultry house, and in the morning there would be feathers lying all over the veranda. Timothy had to be chained up more often. And, finally, when he began to stalk Mahmoud about the house with what looked like villainous intent, Grandfather decided it was time to transfer him to a zoo.

The nearest zoo was at Lucknow, two hundred miles away. Reserving a first-class compartment for himself and Timothy—no one would share a compartment with them—Grandfather took him to Lucknow where the zoo authorities were only too glad to receive as a gift a well-fed and fairly civilized tiger.

About six months later, when my grandparents were visiting relatives in Lucknow, Grandfather took the opportunity of calling at the zoo to see how Timothy was getting on. I was not there to accompany him, but I heard all about it when he returned to Dehra.

Arriving at the zoo, Grandfather made straight for the particular cage in which Timothy had been interned. The tiger was there, crouched in a corner, full-grown and with a magnificent striped coat.

'Hello, Timothy!' said Grandfather and, climbing the railing with ease, he put his arm through the bars of the cage.

The tiger approached the bars and allowed Grandfather to put both hands around his head. Grandfather stroked the tiger's forehead and tickled his ear, and, whenever he growled, smacked him across the mouth, which was his old way of keeping him quiet.

He licked Grandfather's hands and only sprang away when a leopard in the next cage snarled at him. Grandfather 'shooed' the leopard away and the tiger returned to lick his hands; but every now and then the leopard would rush at the bars and the tiger would slink back to his corner.

A number of people had gathered to watch the reunion when a keeper pushed his way through the crowd and asked Grandfather what he was doing.

'I'm talking to Timothy,' said Grandfather. 'Weren't you here when I gave him to the zoo six months ago?'

'I haven't been here very long,' said the surprised keeper. 'Please continue your conversation. But I have never been able to touch him myself, he is always very bad-tempered.'

'Why don't you put him somewhere else?' suggested Grandfather. 'That leopard keeps frightening him. I'll go and see the superintendent about it.'

Grandfather went in search of the superintendent of the zoo, but found that he had gone home early; and so, after wandering about the zoo for a little while, he returned to Timothy's cage to say goodbye. It was beginning to get dark.

He had been stroking and slapping Timothy for about five minutes when he found another keeper observing him with some alarm. Grandfather recognized him as the keeper who had been there when Timothy had first come to the zoo.

'*You* remember me,' said Grandfather. 'Now why don't you transfer Timothy to another cage, away from this stupid leopard?'

'But—sir—' stammered the keeper, 'it is not your tiger.'

'I know, I know,' said Grandfather testily. 'I realize he is no longer mine. But you might at least take a suggestion or two from me.'

'I remember your tiger very well,' said the keeper. 'He died two months ago.'

'Died!' exclaimed Grandfather.

'Yes, sir, of pneumonia. This tiger was trapped in the hills only last month, and he is very dangerous!'

Grandfather could think of nothing to say. The tiger was still licking his arm, with increasing relish. Grandfather took what seemed to him an age to withdraw his hand from the cage.

With his face near the tiger's he mumbled, 'Goodnight, Timothy,' and giving the keeper a scornful look, walked briskly out of the zoo.

GRAN'S KITCHEN

As kitchens went, it wasn't very big. What made it fabulous was all that came out of it. Gran's curries and kebabs, chocolate fudge and peanut toffee, jellies and gulab jamuns, meat pies and apple pies, stuffed chickens, stuffed eggplants, and even ham, stuffed with stuffed chicken! As far as I was concerned, Gran was the best cook in the world.

The town we lived in was called Dehradun. It's still there, though much bigger and more populous since India's independence. Gran had a large, rambling bungalow on the outskirts of town. On the grounds were many fruit trees—mangoes, lichees, guavas, bananas, papayas and lemons—there was room for all of them, including a giant jackfruit tree that threw its shadow on the walls of the house.

Gran had a saying,
'Blessed is the house upon whose walls
The shade of an old tree softly falls.'
She was right, hers was a good house to live in, especially for a ten-year-old boy with a tremendous appetite.

Every winter, when I came home from boarding school, I would spend at least a month with Gran before going over to my parents in Assam. My father managed a tea plantation there, and although the tea gardens were fun to play in, my parents couldn't cook. Like most colonials, they employed a Khansama, a professional cook, who made good mutton curry but little else. So I was always glad to spend half my holidays with Gran.

Gran was glad to have me too, because she lived alone most of the time. Not entirely alone, though. The gardener, his son Mohan and a mongrel dog named Crazy all lived in the compound. And sometimes there was Uncle Ken, a nephew of Gran's, who came to stay whenever he was out of a job (which was fairly often), or when he felt like enjoying some of Gran's cooking.

Gran didn't enjoy cooking just for herself; she liked to have someone to cook for. And although Uncle Ken sometimes appreciated her efforts, and Crazy loved her table scraps, a good cook likes a kid to feed, because kids are adventurous and ready to try even the most unusual dishes.

Whenever Gran tried out a new recipe on me, she would wait for my reaction, and then jot down some of my comments in a notebook. This was useful when she wanted to try the same dish on others.

'Do you like it?' she'd ask, after I'd taken a few mouthfuls.

'Yes, Gran.'

'Sweet enough?'

'Yes, Gran.'

'Not *too* sweet?'

'No, Gran.'

'Would you like some more?'

'Yes please, Gran.'

'Well, finish it off.'

'Mmmm…'

'Eat well, but don't overeat,' Gran used to tell me. And we did eat well, even though all those wonderful meals consisted of only one course followed by a sweet dish. It was Gran's cooking that turned a modest meal into a feast.

Roast duck was one of her specialties. The first time I had

roast duck at Gran's place, Uncle Ken was there too. He'd just lost his job as a railway guard, and had come to stay with Gran until he could find something else.

Uncle Ken ate just as much as I did, but he never praised Gran's dishes and that annoyed me. He looked at the roast duck, his glasses slipping down to the edge of his nose. 'Hmmm… Duck again, Aunt May?'

'What do you mean by duck *again*? We haven't had duck since you were here last month!'

'That's what I mean,' said Uncle Ken. 'Somehow, one expects a little more variety.'

All the same, he took two large helpings and ate most of the stuffing before I could get at it. I got my revenge by emptying all the applesauce onto my plate. Uncle Ken knew I loved stuffing, and I knew he was crazy about Gran's applesauce. So we were even.

Gran was famous all over Dehra for her pickles. Green mangoes, pickled in oil, were always popular. So was her hot lime pickle. And she was adept at pickling turnips, carrots, cauliflowers, and chillies. She could pickle almost any fruit or vegetable—everything from nasturtium seeds to jackfruit.

One winter, when Gran's funds were low, Mohan and I went from house to house…selling pickles for her. Major Clarke, our neighbour across the road, was our first customer.

'And what have you got there?' he asked.

'Pickles, sir.'

'Pickles? Did you make them?'

'No, sir, they're my grandmother's. We're selling them so we can buy a turkey for Christmas.'

'Mrs Bond's pickles, eh? Well, I'm glad this is the first house on your route, because that basket will soon be empty. There's no one who can make a pickle like your grandmother! What have you this time? Stuffed chillies, I hope. She knows they're my favorite. I shall be deeply wounded if there are no stuffed chillies in that basket.'

There were, in fact, three bottles of stuffed red chillies in the basket, and Major Clarke bought all of them.

Further down the road, Dr Dutt bought several bottles of lime pickle, saying it was good for his liver. And Mr Hari, who owned a garage at the end of the road, purchased two bottles of pickled onions and begged us to bring another as soon as we could.

By the time we got home, the basket was empty, and Gran was richer by thirty rupees—enough, in those days, for a turkey.

Uncle Ken stayed for Christmas and ate most of the turkey.

THE NIGHT THE ROOF BLEW OFF

We are used to sudden storms up here on the first range of the Himalayas. The old building in which we live has, for more than a hundred years, received the full force of the wind as it sweeps across the hills from the east.

We'd lived in the building for more than ten years without a disaster. It had even taken the shock of a severe earthquake. As my granddaughter Dolly said, 'It's difficult to tell the new cracks from the old!'

It's a two-storey building, and I live on the upper floor with my family: my three grandchildren and their parents. The roof is made of corrugated tin sheets, the ceiling, of wooden boards. That's the traditional Mussoorie roof.

Looking back at the experience, it was the sort of thing that should have happened in a James Thurber story, like the dam that burst or the ghost who got in. But I wasn't thinking of Thurber at the time, although a few of his books were among the many I was trying to save from the icy rain pouring into my bedroom.

Our roof had held fast in many a storm, but the wind that night was really fierce. It came rushing at us with a high-pitched, eerie wail. The old roof groaned and protested. It took a battering for several hours while the rain lashed against the windows and the lights kept coming and going.

There was no question of sleeping, but we remained in bed

for warmth and comfort. The fire had long since gone out as the chimney had collapsed, bringing down a shower of sooty rainwater.

After about four hours of buffeting, the roof could take it no longer. My bedroom faces east, so my portion of the roof was the first to go.

The wind got under it and kept pushing until, with a ripping, groaning sound, the metal sheets shifted and slid off the rafters, some of them dropping with claps like thunder on to the road below.

So that's it, I thought. Nothing worse can happen. As long as the ceiling stays on, I'm not getting out of bed. We'll collect our roof in the morning.

Icy water splashing down on my face made me change my mind in a hurry. Leaping from the bed, I found that much of the ceiling had gone, too. Water was pouring on my open typewriter as well as on the bedside radio and bed cover.

Picking up my precious typewriter (my companion for forty years) I stumbled into the front sitting room (and library), only to find a similar situation there. Water was pouring through the slats of the wooden ceiling, raining down on the open bookshelves.

By now I had been joined by the children, who had come to my rescue. Their section of the roof hadn't gone as yet. Their parents were struggling to close a window against the driving rain.

'Save the books!' shouted Dolly, the youngest, and that became our rallying cry for the next hour or two.

Dolly and her brother Mukesh picked up armfuls of books and carried them into their room. But the floor was awash, so the books had to be piled on their beds. Dolly was helping me gather some of my papers when a large field rat jumped on to the desk in front of her. Dolly squealed and ran for the door.

'It's all right,' said Mukesh, whose love of animals extends even to field rats. 'It's only sheltering from the storm.'

Big brother Rakesh whistled for our dog, Tony, but Tony wasn't interested in rats just then. He had taken shelter in the kitchen, the only dry spot in the house.

Two rooms were now practically roofless, and we could see the sky lit up by flashes of lightning.

There were fireworks indoors, too, as water spluttered and crackled along a damaged wire. Then the lights went out altogether.

Rakesh, at his best in an emergency, had already lit two kerosene lamps. And by their light we continued to transfer books, papers, and clothes to the children's room.

We noticed that the water on the floor was beginning to subside a little.

'Where is it going?' asked Dolly.

'Through the floor,' said Mukesh. 'Down to the flat below!'

Cries of concern from our downstairs neighbours told us that they were having their share of the flood.

Our feet were freezing because there hadn't been time to put on proper footwear. And besides, shoes and slippers were awash by now. All chairs and tables were piled high with books. I hadn't realized the extent of my library until that night!

The available beds were pushed into the driest corner of the children's room, and there, huddled in blankets and quilts, we spent the remaining hours of the night while the storm continued.

Towards morning the wind fell, and it began to snow. Through the door to the sitting room I could see snowflakes drifting through the gaps in the ceiling, settling on picture frames. Ordinary things like a glue bottle and a small clock took on a certain beauty when covered with soft snow.

Most of us dozed off.

When dawn came, we found the windowpanes encrusted with snow and icicles. The rising sun struck through the gaps in the ceiling and turned everything golden. Snow crystals glistened on the empty bookshelves. But the books had been saved.

Rakesh went out to find a carpenter and tinsmith, while the rest of us started putting things in the sun to dry. By evening, we'd put much of the roof back on.

It's a much-improved roof now, and we look forward to the next storm with confidence!

GRANNY'S PROVERBS

A hungry man is an angry man,
Said dear old Gran
As she prepared an Irish stew
For the chosen few
(Gran'dad, my cousins and me).
But then she'd turn to me and emote—
'Don't be greedy, or your tongue will cut your throat!'
'And if I asked for more of my favourite fish,
'That small fish,' she'd say, 'is better than an empty dish!'
Like Mann, she taught us to honour our food,
She was the law-giver, seeking all good.
Gran'dad and I, we'd eat what we were given
(Irish stew and a tart)
But sometimes we'd sneak away to the bazaar
To feast on tikkees and chaat
—And that was heaven!

(You can read more about my grandparents in 'Grandfather's Private Zoo' in
my children's omnibus.)

ALL CREATURES GREAT AND SMALL

Instead of having brothers and sisters to grow up with in India, I had as my companions an odd assortment of pets, which included a monkey, a tortoise, a python and a Great Indian Hornbill. The person responsible for all this wildlife in the home was my grandfather. As the house was his own, other members of the family could not prevent him from keeping a large variety of pets, though they could certainly voice their objections; and as most of the household consisted of women—my grandmother, visiting aunts and occasional in-laws (my parents were in Burma at the time)—Grandfather and I had to be alert and resourceful in dealing with them. We saw eye to eye on the subject of pets, and whenever Grandmother decided it was time to get rid of a tame white rat or a squirrel, I would conceal them in a hole in the jackfruit tree; but unlike my aunts, she was generally tolerant of Grandfather's hobby, and even took a liking to some of our pets.

Grandfather's house and menagerie were in Dehra and I remember travelling there in a horse-drawn buggy. There were cars in those days—it was just over twenty years ago—but in the foothills a tonga was just as good, almost as fast, and certainly more dependable when it came to getting across the swift little Tons river.

During the rains, when the river flowed strong and deep, it was impossible to get across except on a hand-operated ropeway; but in the dry months, the horse went splashing through, the carriage wheels churning through clear mountain water. If the horse found the going difficult, we removed our shoes, rolled up our skirts or trousers, and waded across.

When Grandfather first went to stay in Dehra, early in the century, the only way of getting there was by the night mail coach.

Mail ponies, he told me, were difficult animals, always attempting to turn around and get into the coach with the passengers. It was only when the coachman used his whip liberally, and reviled the ponies' ancestors as far back as their third and fourth generations, that the beasts could be persuaded to move. And once they started, there was no stopping them. It was a gallop all the way to the first stage, where the ponies were changed to the accompaniment of a bugle blown by the coachman.

At one stage of the journey, drums were beaten; and if it was night, torches were lit to keep away the wild elephants who, resenting the approach of this clumsy caravan, would sometimes trumpet a challenge and throw the ponies into confusion.

Grandfather disliked dressing up and going out, and was only too glad to send everyone shopping or to the pictures— Harold Lloyd and Eddie Cantor were the favourites at Dehra's small cinema—so that he could be left alone to feed his pets and potter about in the garden. There were a lot of animals to be fed, including, for a time, a pair of Great Danes who had such enormous appetites that we were forced to give them away to a more affluent family.

The Great Danes were gentle creatures, and I would sit astride one of them and go for rides round the garden. In spite of their size, they were very sure-footed and never knocked over people or chairs. A little monkey, like Toto, did much more damage.

Grandfather bought Toto from a tonga owner for the sum of five rupees. The tonga man used to keep the little red monkey tied to a feeding trough, and Toto looked so out of place there—almost conscious of his own incongruity—that Grandfather immediately decided to add him to our menagerie.

Toto was really a pretty little monkey. His bright eyes sparkled with mischief beneath deep-set eyebrows, and his teeth, a pearly-white, were often on display in a smile that frightened the life out of elderly Anglo-Indian ladies. His hands were not those of a Tallulah Bankhead (Grandfather's only favourite actress), but were shrivelled and dried-up, as though they had been pickled in the sun for many years. But his fingers were quick and restless; and his tail, while adding to his good looks— Grandfather maintained that a tail would add to anyone's good looks—often performed the service of a third hand. He could use it to hang from a branch; and it was capable of scooping up any delicacy that might be out of reach of his hands.

Grandmother, anticipating an outcry from other relatives, always raised objections when Grandfather brought home some new bird or animal, and so for a while we managed to keep Toto's presence a secret by lodging him in a little closet opening into my bedroom wall. But in a few hours he managed to dispose of Grandmother's ornamental wallpaper and the better part of my school blazer. He was transferred to the stables for a day or two, and then Grandfather had to make a trip to neighbouring Saharanpur to collect his railway pension and, anxious to keep Toto out of trouble, he decided to take the monkey along with him.

Unfortunately, I could not accompany Grandfather on this trip, but he told me about it afterwards.

A black kitbag was provided for Toto. When the strings of the bag were tied, there was no means of escape from within, and the canvas was too strong for Toto to bite his way through. His initial efforts to get out only had the effect of making the bag roll about on the floor, or occasionally jump in the air—an exhibition that attracted a curious crowd of onlookers on the Dehra railway platform.

Toto remained in the bag as far as Saharanpur, but while Grandfather was producing his ticket at the railway turnstile, Toto managed to get his hands through the aperture where the bag was tied, loosened the strings, and suddenly thrust his head through the opening.

The poor ticket collector was visibly alarmed; but with great presence of mind, and much to the annoyance of Grandfather, he said, 'Sir, you have a dog with you. You'll have to pay for it accordingly.'

In vain did Grandfather take Toto out of the bag to prove that a monkey was not a dog or even a quadruped. The ticket collector, now thoroughly annoyed, insisted on classing Toto as a dog; and three rupees and four annas had to be handed over as his fare. Then Grandfather, out of sheer spite, took out from his pocket a live tortoise that he happened to have with him, and said, 'What must I pay for this, since you charge for all animals?'

The ticket collector retreated a pace or two; then advancing again with caution, he subjected the tortoise to a grave and knowledgeable stare.

'No ticket is necessary, sir,' he finally declared. 'There is no charge for insects.'

When we discovered that Toto's favourite pastime was catching mice, we were able to persuade Grandmother to let us keep him. The unsuspecting mice would emerge from their holes at night to pick up any corn left over by our pony; and to get at it they had to run the gauntlet of Toto's section of the stable. He knew this, and would pretend to be asleep, keeping, however, one eye open. A mouse would make a rush—in vain; Toto, as swift as a cat, would have his paws upon him.

Grandmother decided to put his talents to constructive use by tying him up one night in the larder, where a guerrilla band of mice were playing havoc with our food supplies.

Toto was removed from his comfortable bed of straw in the stable, and chained up in the larder, beneath shelves of jam pots and other delicacies. The night was a long and miserable one for Toto, who must have wondered what he had done to deserve such treatment. The mice scampered about the place, while he, most uncat-like, lay curled up in a soup tureen, trying to snatch some sleep. At dawn, the mice returned to their holes; Toto awoke, scratched himself, emerged from the soup tureen, and looked about for something to eat. The jam pots attracted his notice, and it did not take him long to prise open the covers. Grandmother's treasured jams—she had made most of them herself—disappeared in an amazingly short time. I was present when she opened the door to see how many mice Toto had caught. Even the rain god, Indra, could not have looked more terrible when planning a thunderstorm; and the imprecations Grandmother hurled at Toto were surprising coming from someone who had been brought up in the genteel Victorian manner.

The monkey was later reinstated in Grandmother's favour. A great treat for him on cold winter evenings was the large bowl of warm water provided by Grandmother for his bath. He would bathe himself, first of all gingerly testing the temperature of the water with his fingers. Leisurely, he would step into the bath, first one foot, then the other, as he had seen me doing, until he was completely sitting down in it. Once comfortable, he would take the soap in his hands or feet, and rub himself all over. When he found the water becoming cold, he would get out and run as quickly as he could to the fire, where his coat soon dried. If anyone laughed at him during this performance, he would look extremely hurt, and refuse to go on with his ablutions.

One day Toto nearly succeeded in boiling himself to death. The large kitchen kettle had been left on the fire to boil for tea; and Toto, finding himself for a few minutes alone with it, decided to take the lid off. On discovering that the water inside was warm, he got into the kettle with the intention of having a bath, and sat down with his head protruding from the opening. This was very pleasant for some time, until the water began to simmer. Toto raised himself a little, but finding it cold outside, sat down again. He continued standing and sitting for some time, not having the courage to face the cold air. Had it not been for the timely arrival of Grandmother, he would have been cooked alive.

If there is a part of the brain especially devoted to mischief, that part must have been largely developed in Toto. He was always tearing things to bits, and whenever one of my aunts came near him, he made every effort to get hold of her dress and tear a hole in it. A variety of aunts frequently came to stay with my grandparents, but during Toto's stay they limited their visits to a day or two, much to Grandfather's relief and Grandmother's annoyance.

Toto, however, took a liking to Grandmother, in spite of the beatings he often received from her. Whenever she allowed him the liberty, he would lie quietly in her lap instead of scrambling all over her as he did on most people.

Toto lived with us over a year, but the following winter, after too much bathing, he caught pneumonia. Grandmother wrapped him in flannel, and Grandfather gave him a diet of chicken soup and Irish stew; but Toto did not recover. He was buried in the garden, under his favourite mango tree.

Perhaps it was just as well that Toto was no longer with us when Grandfather brought home the python, or his demise might have been less conventional. Small monkeys are a favourite delicacy with pythons.

Grandmother was tolerant of most birds and animals, but she drew the line at reptiles. She said they made her blood run cold. Even a handsome, sweet-tempered chameleon had to be given up. Grandfather should have known that there was little chance of his being allowed to keep the python. It was about four feet long, a young one, when Grandfather bought it from a snake charmer for six rupees, impressing the bazaar crowd by slinging it across his shoulders and walking home with it. Grandmother nearly fainted at the sight of the python curled round Grandfather's throat.

'You'll be strangled!' she cried. 'Get rid of it at once!'

'Nonsense,' said Grandfather. 'He's only a young fellow. He'll soon get used to us.'

'Will he, indeed?' said Grandmother. 'But I have no intention of getting used to him. You know quite well that your cousin Mabel is coming to stay with us tomorrow. She'll leave us the minute she knows there's a snake in the house.'

'Well, perhaps we ought to show it to her as soon as she arrives,' said Grandfather, who did not look forward to fussy Aunt Mabel's visits any more than I did.

'You'll do no such thing,' said Grandmother.

'Well, I can't let it loose in the garden,' said Grandfather with an innocent expression. 'It might find its way into the poultry house, and then where would we be?'

'How exasperating you are!' grumbled Grandmother. 'Lock the creature in the bathroom, go back to the bazaar and find the man you bought it from, and get him to come and take it back.'

In my awestruck presence, Grandfather had to take the python into the bathroom, where he placed it in a steep-sided tin tub. Then he hurried off to the bazaar to look for the snake charmer, while Grandmother paced anxiously up and down the veranda. When he returned looking crestfallen, we knew he hadn't been able to find the man.

'You had better take it away yourself,' said Grandmother, in a relentless mood. 'Leave it in the jungle across the riverbed.'

'All right, but let me give it a feed first,' said Grandfather; and producing a plucked chicken, he took it into the bathroom, followed, in single file, by me, Grandmother and a curious cook and gardener.

Grandfather threw open the door and stepped into the bathroom. I peeped round his legs, while the others remained well behind. We couldn't see the python anywhere.

'He's gone,' announced Grandfather. 'He must have felt hungry.'

'I hope he isn't too hungry,' I said.

'We left the window open,' said Grandfather, looking embarrassed.

A careful search was made of the house, the kitchen, the garden, the stable and the poultry shed; but the python couldn't be found anywhere.

'He'll be well away by now,' said Grandfather reassuringly.

'I certainly hope so,' said Grandmother, who was half way between anxiety and relief.

Aunt Mabel arrived next day for a three-week visit, and for a couple of days Grandfather and I were a little apprehensive, in case the python made a sudden reappearance; but on the third day, when he didn't show up, we felt confident that he had gone for good.

And then, towards evening, we were startled by a scream from the garden. Seconds later, Aunt Mabel came flying up the veranda steps, looking as though she had seen a ghost.

'In the guava tree!' she gasped. 'I was reaching for a guava, when I saw it staring at me. The look in its eyes! As though it would devour me—'

'Calm down, my dear,' urged Grandmother, sprinkling her with eau-de-cologne. 'Calm down and tell us what you saw.'

'A snake!' sobbed Aunt Mabel. 'A great boa constrictor. It must have been twenty feet long! In the guava tree. Its eyes were terrible. It looked at me in such a queer way...'

My grandparents looked significantly at each other, and Grandfather said, 'I'll go out and kill it,' and sheepishly taking hold of an umbrella, sallied out into the garden. But when he reached the guava tree, the python had disappeared.

'Aunt Mabel must have frightened it away,' I said.

'Hush,' said Grandfather. 'We mustn't speak of your aunt in that way.' But his eyes were alive with laughter.

After this incident, the python began to make a series of appearances, often in the most unexpected places. Aunt Mabel had another fit of hysterics when she saw him admiring her from under a cushion. She packed her bags, and Grandmother made us intensify the hunt.

Next morning, I saw the python curled up on the dressing table, gazing at his reflection in the mirror. I went for Grandfather, but by the time we returned the python had moved elsewhere. A little later he was seen in the garden again. Then he was back on the dressing table, admiring himself in the mirror. Evidently he had become enamoured of his own reflection. Grandfather observed that perhaps the attention he was receiving from everyone had made him a little conceited.

'He's trying to look better for Aunt Mabel,' I said; a remark that I instantly regretted, because Grandmother overheard it, and brought the flat of her broad hand down on my head.

'Well, now we know his weakness,' said Grandfather.

'Are you trying to be funny too?' demanded Grandmother, looking her most threatening.

'I only meant he was becoming very vain,' said Grandfather hastily. 'It should be easier to catch him now.'

He set about preparing a large cage with a mirror at one end. In the cage he left a juicy chicken and various other delicacies, and fitted up the opening with a trapdoor. Aunt Mabel had already left by the time we had this trap ready, but we had to go on with the project because we couldn't have the python prowling about the house indefinitely.

For a few days nothing happened, and then, as I was leaving for school one morning, I saw the python curled up in the cage. He had eaten everything left out for him, and was relaxing in front of the mirror with something resembling a smile on his face—if you can imagine a python smiling… I lowered the trapdoor gently, but the python took no notice; he was in raptures over his handsome reflection. Grandfather and the gardener put the cage in the ponytrap, and made a journey to the other side of the riverbed. They left the cage in the jungle, with the trapdoor open.

'He made no attempt to get out,' said Grandfather later. 'And I didn't have the heart to take the mirror away. It's the first time I've seen a snake fall in love.'

'And the frogs have sung their old song in the mud…' This was Grandfather's favourite quotation from Virgil, and he used it whenever we visited the rainwater pond behind the house where there were quantities of mud and frogs and the occasional water buffalo. Grandfather had once brought a number of frogs into the house. He had put them in a glass jar, left them on a windowsill, and then forgotten all about them. At about four o'clock in the morning the entire household was awakened by a loud and fearful noise, and Grandmother and several nervous relatives gathered in their nightclothes on the veranda. Their timidity changed to fury when they discovered that the ghastly sounds had come from Grandfather's frogs. Seeing the dawn breaking, the frogs had with one accord begun their morning song.

Grandmother wanted to throw the frogs, bottle and all, out of the window; but Grandfather said that if he gave the bottle a good shaking, the frogs would remain quiet. He was obliged to keep awake, in order to shake the bottle whenever the frogs showed any inclination to break into song. Fortunately for all concerned, the next day a servant took the top off the bottle to see what was inside. The sight of several big frogs so startled him that he ran off without replacing the cover; the frogs jumped out and presumably found their way back to the pond.

It became a habit with me to visit the pond on my own, in order to explore its banks and shallows. Taking off my shoes, I would wade into the muddy water up to my knees, to pluck the water lilies that floated on the surface.

One day I found the pond already occupied by several buffaloes. Their keeper, a boy a little older than me, was swimming about in the middle. Instead of climbing out on to the bank, he would pull himself up on the back of one of his buffaloes, stretch his naked brown body out on the animal's glistening wet hide, and start singing to himself.

When he saw me staring at him from across the pond, he smiled, showing gleaming white teeth in a dark, sun-burnished face. He invited me to join him in a swim. I told him I couldn't swim, and he offered to teach me. I hesitated, knowing that Grandmother held strict and old-fashioned views about mixing with village children; but, deciding that Grandfather— who sometimes smoked a hookah on the sly—would get me out of any trouble that might occur, I took the bold step of accepting the boy's offer. Once taken, the step did not seem so bold.

He dived off the back of his buffalo, and swam across to

me. And I, having removed my clothes, followed his instructions until I was floundering about among the water lilies. His name was Ramu, and he promised to give me swimming lessons every afternoon; and so it was during the afternoon—especially summer afternoons when everyone was asleep—that we usually met. Before long I was able to swim across the pond to sit with Ramu astride a contented buffalo, the great beast standing like an island in the middle of a muddy ocean.

Sometimes we would try racing the buffaloes, Ramu and I sitting on different mounts. But they were lazy creatures, and would leave one comfortable spot only to look for another; or, if they were in no mood for games, would roll over on their backs, taking us with them into the mud and green slime of the pond. Emerging in shades of green and khaki, I would slip into the house through the bathroom and bathe under the tap before getting into my clothes.

One afternoon, Ramu and I found a small tortoise in the mud, sitting over a hole in which it had laid several eggs. Ramu kept the eggs for his dinner, and I presented the tortoise to Grandfather. He had a weakness for tortoises, and was pleased with this addition to his menagerie, giving it a large tub of water all to itself, with an island of rocks in the middle. The tortoise, however, was always getting out of the tub and wandering about the house. As it seemed able to look after itself quite well, we did not interfere. If one of the dogs bothered it too much, it would draw its head and legs into its shell and defy all their attempts at rough play.

Ramu came from a family of bonded labourers, and had received no schooling. But he was well-versed in folklore, and knew a great deal about birds and animals.

'Many birds are sacred,' said Ramu, as we watched a blue jay swoop down from a peepul tree and carry off a grasshopper. He told me that both the blue jay and the God Shiva were called 'Nilkanth'. Shiva had a blue throat, like the bird, because out of compassion for the human race he had swallowed a deadly poison which was intended to destroy the world. Keeping the poison in his throat, he did not let it go any further.

'Are squirrels sacred?' I asked, seeing one sprint down the trunk of the peepul tree.

'Oh, yes, Lord Krishna loved squirrels,' said Ramu. 'He would take them in his arms and stroke them with his long fingers. That is why they have four dark lines down their backs from head to tail. Krishna was very dark, and the lines are the marks of his fingers.'

Both Ramu and Grandfather were of the opinion that we should be more gentle with birds and animals and should not kill so many of them.

'It is also important that we respect them,' said Grandfather. 'We must acknowledge their rights. Everywhere, birds and animals are finding it more difficult to survive, because we are trying to destroy both them and their forests. They have to keep moving as the trees disappear.'

This was especially true of the forests near Dehra, where the tiger and the pheasant and the spotted deer were beginning to disappear.

Ramu and I spent many long summer afternoons at the pond. I still remember him with affection, though we never saw each other again after I left Dehra. He could not read or write, so we were unable to keep in touch. And neither his people, nor mine, knew of our friendship. The buffaloes and frogs had been our only confidantes. They had accepted us as part of their own world, their muddy but comfortable pond. And when I left Dehra, both they and Ramu must have assumed that I would return again like the birds.

THE EARTHQUAKE

'If ever there's a calamity,' Grandmother used to say, 'it will find Grandfather in his bath.' Grandfather loved his bath—which he took in a large round aluminum tub—and sometimes spent as long as an hour in it, 'wallowing' as he called it, and splashing around like a boy.

He was in his bath during the earthquake that convulsed Bengal and Assam on 12 June 1897—an earthquake so severe that even today, the region of the great Brahmaputra river basin hasn't settled down. Not long ago, it was reported that the entire Shillong Plateau had moved an appreciable distance away from the Geological Survey of India; this shift has been taking place gradually over the past eighty years.

Had Grandfather been alive, he would have added one more clipping to his scrapbook on earthquakes. The clipping goes in anyway, because the scrapbook is now with his children. More than newspaper accounts of the disaster, it was Grandfather's own letters and memoirs that made the earthquake seem recent and vivid; for he, along with Grandmother and two of their children (one of them my father), was living in Shillong, a picturesque little hill station in Assam, when the earth shook and the mountains heaved.

As I have mentioned, Grandfather was in his bath, splashing about, and did not hear the first rumbling. But Grandmother was in the garden hanging out or taking in the washing (she could never remember which) when, suddenly, the animals began making a hideous noise—a sure intimation of a natural disaster, for animals sense the approach of an earthquake much more quickly than humans.

The crows all took wing, wheeling wildly overhead and cawing loudly. The chickens flapped in circles, as if they were being chased. Two dogs sitting on the verandah suddenly jumped up and ran out with their tails between their legs. Within half a minute of her noticing the noise made by the animals, Grandmother heard a rattling, rumbling noise, like the approach of a train.

The noise increased for about a minute, and then there was the first trembling of the ground. The animals by this time all seemed to have gone mad. Treetops lashed backwards and forwards, doors banged and windows shook, and Grandmother swore later that the house actually swayed in front of her. She had difficulty in standing straight, though this could have been more due to the trembling of her knees than to the trembling of the ground.

The first shock lasted for about a minute and a half. 'I was in my tub having a bath,' Grandfather wrote for posterity, 'which for the first time in the last two months I had taken in the afternoon instead of in the morning. My wife and children and the maid were downstairs. Then the shock came and a quaking, which increased in intensity every second. It was like putting so many shells in a basket, and shaking them up with a rapid sifting motion from side to side.

'At first I did not realize what it was that caused my tub to sway about and the water to splash. I rose up, and found the earth heaving, while the washstand basin, ewer, cups and glasses danced and rocked about in the most hideous fashion. I rushed to the inner door to open it and search for my wife and children but could not move the dratted door as boxes, furniture and plaster had come up against it. The back door was the only way of escape. I managed to open it and, thank God, was able to get out. All the sections of the thatched roof had slithered down on the four sides like a pack of cards and blocked all the exits and entrances.

'With only a towel wrapped around my waist, I ran into the open to the front of the house, but found only my wife there. The whole front of the house was blocked by the fallen section of thatch from the roof. Through this I broke my way under the iron railings and extricated the others. The bearer had pluckily borne the weight of the whole thatched roof section on his back, and in this way saved the maid and children from being crushed beneath it.'

After the main shock of the earthquake had passed, minor shocks took place at regular intervals of five minutes or so, all through the night. But during that first shakeup, the town of Shillong was reduced to ruin and rubble. Everything made of masonry was brought to the ground. Government House, the post office, the jail, all tumbled down. When the jail fell, the prisoners, instead of making their escape, sat huddled on the road waiting for the superintendent to come to their aid.

'The ground began to heave and shake,' wrote a young girl in a newspaper called *The Englishman*. 'I stayed on my bicycle for a second, and then fell off and got up and tried to run, staggering about from side to side of the road. To my left I saw great clouds of dust, which I afterwards discovered to be houses falling and the earth slipping from the sides of the hills. To my right I saw the small dam at the end of the lake torn asunder and the water rushing out, the wooden bridge across the lake break in two and the sides of the lake falling in; and at my feet, the ground cracking and opening. I was wild with fear and didn't know which way to turn.'

The lake rose up like a mountain, and then totally disappeared, leaving only a swamp of red mud. Not a house was left standing. People were rushing about, wives looking for husbands, parents looking for children, not knowing whether their loved ones were alive or dead. A crowd of people had collected on the cricket ground, which was considered the safest place; but Grandfather and the family took shelter in a small shop on the road outside his house. The shop was a rickety wooden structure, which had always looked as though it would fall down in a strong wind. But it withstood the earthquake.

And then the rain came and it poured. This was extraordinary, because before the earthquake there wasn't a cloud to be seen; but five minutes after, the shock was felt for more than a hundred miles on the Assam-Bengal Railway. A train overturned at Shamshernagar; another was derailed at Mantolla. Over a thousand people lost lives in the Cherrapunji Hills, and in other areas, too, the death toll was heavy.

The Brahmaputra burst its banks and many cultivators were drowned in the flood. A tiger was found drowned. And in North Bhagalpur, where the earthquake started, two elephants sat down in the bazaar and refused to get up until the following morning.

Over a hundred men, who were at work in Shillong's government printing press, were caught in the building when it collapsed, and though the men of Gurkha regiment did splendid rescue work, only a few were brought out alive. One of those killed in Shillong was Mr McCabe, a British official. Grandfather described the ruins of Mr McCabe's house: 'Here a bedpost, there a sword, a broken desk or chair, a bit of torn carpet, a well-known hat with its Indian Civil Service colours, battered books, speaking reminiscenes of the man we mourn.'

While most houses collapsed where they stood, Government House, it seems, fell backwards. The church was a mass of red stones in an ugly disorder. The organ was a tortured wreck.

A few days later, the family, with other refugees, were making their way to Calcutta to stay with friends or relatives. It was a slow, tedious journey with many interruptions, for the roads and railway lines had been badly damaged, and passengers had often to be transported in trolleys. Grandfather was rather struck at the stoicism displayed by an assistant engineer. At one station, a telegram was handed to the engineer informing him that his bungalow had been destroyed. 'Beastly nuisance,' he observed with an aggrieved air. 'I've seen it cave in during a storm, but this is the first time it has played me such a trick on account of an earthquake.'

The family got to Calcutta to find the inhabitants of the capital in a panic; for they too had felt the quake and were expecting it to recur. The damage in Calcutta was slight compared to the devastation elsewhere, but nerves were on the edge, and people slept in the open or in carriages. Cracks and fissures had appeared in a number of old buildings, and Grandfather was among the many who were worried at the proposal to fire a salute of sixty guns on Jubilee Day (the Diamond Jubilee of Queen Victoria). They felt the gunfire would bring down a number of shaky buildings. Obviously Grandfather did not wish to be caught in his bath a second time. However, Queen Victoria was not to be deprived of her salute. The guns were duly fired, and Calcutta remained standing.

GRANNY'S TREE-CLIMBING

Granny was a genius. You'd like to know why?
Because she could climb trees. Spreading or high,
She'd be up their branches in a trice. And mind you,
When last she climbed a tree she was sixty-two.

Ever since childhood, she'd had this gift
For being happier in a tree than in a lift;
And though, as time went by, she would be told
That climbing trees should stop when one grew old—
And that growing old should be gone about gracefully—
She'd laugh and say, 'Well, I'll grow old disgracefully!
I can do it better.' And we had to agree;
For in all the garden there wasn't a tree
She hadn't been up at one time or another—
(Having learned to climb from a loving brother
When she was six)—but it was feared by all
That one day she'd suffer a terrible fall.

The outcome was different—while we were in town
She climbed a tree and couldn't come down!
She remained on her perch until we came home,
We fetched her a ladder, and she came down alone.

As she looked a bit shaken, we sent for out doc,
Who said, 'She is fine—just a bit of a shock.'

He took Granny's temperature. 'Some fever,' he said;
'I strongly recommend a quiet week in bed.'

We sighed with relief and tucked her up well—
Poor Granny! It was just like a season in hell:
Confined to her bedroom, while every breeze
Murmured of summer and dancing leaves...
But she held her peace till she felt stronger,
Then sat up and said, 'I'll lie here no longer!'
She called for my father and told him undaunted
That a house in a tree-top was what she now wanted.
My Dad knew his duty. He said, 'That's all right—
'You'll have what you want—I shall start work tonight.'

With my expert assistance, he soon finished the chore,
Made her a tree-house with windows and a door.
So Granny moved up; and now, everyday,
I go to her room with glasses and a tray.
She sits there in state and drinks cocktails with me,
Upholding her right to reside in a tree.

[Written for Grandmothers' Rights Everywhere]

A WALK THROUGH GARHWAL

I wake to what sounds like the din of a factory buzzer, but is in fact the music of a single vociferous cicada in the lime tree near my window.

Through the open window, I focus on a pattern of small, glossy lime leaves; then through them I see the mountains, the Himalayas, striding away into an immensity of sky.

'In a thousand ages of the gods I could not tell thee of the glories of Himachal.' So confessed a Sanskrit poet at the dawn of Indian history and he came closer than anyone else to capturing the spell of the Himalayas. The sea has had Conrad and Stevenson and Masefield, but the mountains continue to defy the written word. We have climbed their highest peaks and crossed their most difficult passes, but still they keep their secrets and their reserve; they remain remote, mysterious, spirit-haunted.

No wonder then, that the people who live on the mountain slopes in the mist-filled valleys of Garhwal, have long since learned humility, patience and a quiet resignation. Deep in the crouching mist lie their villages, while climbing the mountain slopes are forests of rhododendron, spruce and deodar, soughing in the wind from the ice-bound passes. Pale women plough, they laugh at the thunder as their men go down to the plains for work; for little grows on the beautiful mountains in the north wind.

When I think of Manjari village in Garhwal I see a small river, a tributary of the Ganga, rushing along the bottom of a steep, rocky valley. On the banks of the river and on the terraced hills above, there are small fields of corn, barley, mustard, potatoes and onions. A few fruit trees grow near the village. Some hillsides are rugged and bare, just masses of quartz or granite. On hills exposed to wind, only grass and small shrubs are able to obtain a foothold.

This landscape is typical of Garhwal, one of India's most northerly regions with its massive snow ranges bordering on Tibet. Although thinly populated, it does not provide much of a living for its people. Most Garliwali cultivators are poor, some are very poor. 'You have beautiful scenery,' I observed after crossing the first range of hills.

'Yes,' said my friend, 'but we cannot eat the scenery.'

And yet these are cheerful people, sturdy and with wonderful powers of endurance. Somehow they manage to wrest a precarious living from the unhelpful, calcinated soil. I am their guest for a few days.

My friend Gajadhar has brought me to his home, to his village above the little Nayar river. We took a train into the foothills and then we took a bus and finally, made dizzy by the hairpin bends devised in the last century by a brilliantly diabolical road-engineer, we alighted at the small hill station of Lansdowne, chief recruiting centre for the Garhwal Regiment.

Lansdowne is just over six thousand feet high. From there we walked, covering twenty-five miles between sunrise and sunset, until we came to Manjari village, clinging to the terraced slopes of a very proud, very permanent mountain.

And this is my fourth morning in the village.

Other mornings I was woken by the throaty chuckles of the red-billed blue magpies, as they glided between oak trees and medlars; but today the cicada has drowned all bird song. It is a little out of season for cicadas but perhaps this sudden warm spell in late September has deceived him into thinking it is mating season again.

Early though it is, I am the last to get up. Gajadhar is exercising in the courtyard, going through an odd combination of Swedish exercises and yoga. He has a fine physique with the sturdy legs that most Garhwalis possess. I am sure he will realize his ambition of joining the Indian Army as a cadet. His younger brother Chakradhar, who is slim and fair with high cheekbones, is milking the family's buffalo. Normally, he would be on his long walk to school, five miles distant; but this is a holiday, so he can stay at home and help with the household chores.

His mother is lighting a fire. She is a handsome woman even though her ears, weighed clown by heavy silver earrings have lost their natural shape. Garhwali women usually invest their savings in silver ornaments. And at the time of marriage, it is the boy's parents who make a gift of land to the parents of an attractive girl; a dowry system in reverse. There are fewer women than men in the hills and their good looks and sturdy physique give them considerable status among the men-folk.

Chakradhar's father is a corporal in the Indian Army and is away for most of the year.

When Gajadhar marries, his wife will stay in the village to help his mother and younger brother look after the fields, house, goats and buffalo. Gajadhar will see her only when he comes home on leave. He prefers it that way; he does not think a simple hill girl should be exposed to the sophisticated temptations of the plains.

The village is far above the river and most of the fields depend on rainfall. But water must be fetched for cooking, washing and drinking. And so, after a breakfast of hot sweet milk and thick *chajmaues* stuffed with minced radish, the brothers and I set off down the rough track to the river.

The still has climbed the mountains but it has yet to reach

the narrow valley. We bathe in the river, Gajadhar and Chakradhar dive off a massive rock; but I wade in circumspectly, unfamiliar with the river's depths and currents. The water, a milky blue has come from the melting snows; it is very cold. I bathe quickly and then dash for a strip of sand where a little sunshine has split down the mountainside in warm, golden pools of light. At the same time the song of the whistling-thrush emerges like a dark secret from the wooded shadows. A little later, buckets filled, we toil up the steep mountain. We must go by a better path this time if we are not to come tumbling down with our buckets of water. As we climb, we are mocked by a barbet which sits high up in a spruce calling feverishly in its monotonous mournful way.

'We call it the mewli bird,' says Gajadhar, 'there is a story about it. People say that the souls of men who have suffered injuries in the law courts of the plains and who have died of their disappointments, transmigrate into the mewli birds. That is why the birds are always crying *un, raee-oru, un nee ow,* which means "injustice, injustice!"'

The path leads us past a primary school, a small temple, and a single shop in which it is possible to buy salt, soap and a few other necessities. It is also the post office. And today it is serving as a lock-up.

The villagers have apprehended a local thief, who specializes in stealing jewellery from women while they are working in the fields. He is awaiting escort to the Lansdowne police station, and the shop-keeper-cum-postmaster-cum-constable brings him out for us to inspect. He is a mild-looking fellow, clearly shy of the small crowd that has gathered round him. I wonder how he manages to deprive the strong hill-women of their jewellery; it could not be by force! Any cases of crimes and violence are rare in Garhwal; and robbery too, is uncommon for the simple reason that there is very little to rob.

The thief is rather glad of my presence, as it distracts attention from him. Strangers seldom come to Manjari. The crowd leaves him, turns to me, eager to catch a glimpse of the stranger in its midst. The children exclaim, point at me with delight, chatter among themselves. I might be a visitor from another planet instead of just an itinerant writer from the plains.

The postman has yet to arrive. The mail is brought in relays from Lansdowne. The Manjari postman who has to cover eight miles and delivers letters at several small villages on his route, should arrive around noon. He also serves as a newspaper, bringing the villagers news of the outside world. Over the years he has acquired a reputation for being highly inventive, sometimes creating his own news; so much so that when he told the villagers that men had landed on the moon, no one believed him. There are still a few sceptics.

Gajadhar has been walking out of the village every day, anxious to meet the postman. He is expecting a letter giving the results of his army entrance examination. If he is successful he will be called for an interview. And then, if he is accepted, he will be trained as an officer-cadet. After two years he will become a second lieutenant. His father, after twelve years in the army is still only a corporal. But his father never went to school. There were no schools in the hills during his father's youth.

The Manjari school is only up to class five and it has about forty pupils. If these children (most of them boys) want to study any further, then, like Chakradhar, they must walk the five miles to the high school at the next big village.

'Don't you get tired walking ten miles every day?' I ask Chakradhar.

'I am used to it,' he says. 'I like walking.'

I know that he only has two meals a day—one at seven in the morning when he leaves home and the other at six or seven in the evening when he returns from school—and I ask him if he does not get hungry on the way.

'There is always the wild fruit,' he replies.

It appears that he is an expert on wild fruit: the purple berries of the thorny bilberry bushes ripening in May and June; wild strawberries like drops of blood on the dark green monsoon grass; small sour cherries and tough medlars in the winter months. Chakradhar's strong teeth and probing tongue extract whatever tang or sweetness lies hidden in them. And in March there are the rhododendron flowers. His mother makes them into jam. But Chakradhar likes them as they are: he places the petals on his tongue and chews till the sweet juice trickles down his throat.

He has never been ill.

'But what happens when someone is ill?' I ask knowing that in Manjari there are no medicines, no dispensary or hospital.

'He goes to bed until he is better,' says Gajadhar. 'We have a few home remedies. But if someone is very sick, we carry the person to the hospital at Lansdowne.' He pauses as though wondering how much he should say, then shrugs and says: 'Last year my uncle was very ill. He had a terrible pain in his stomach. For two days he cried out with the pain. So we made a litter and started out for Lansdowne. We had already carried him fifteen miles when he died. And then we had to carry him back again.'

Some of the villages have dispensaries managed by compounders but the remoter areas of Garhwal are completely without medical aid. To the outsider, life in the Garhwal hills may seem idyllic and the people simple. But the Garhwali is far from being simple and his life is one long struggle, especially if he happens to be living in a high altitude village snowbound for four months in the year, with cultivation coming to a standstill and people having to manage with the food gathered and stored during the summer months.

Fortunately, the clear mountain air and the simple diet keep the Garhwalis free from most diseases, and help them recover from the more common ailments. The greatest dangers come from unexpected disasters, such as an accident with an axe or scythe, or an attack by a wild animal. A few years back, several Manjari children and old women were killed by a man-eating leopard. The leopard was finally killed by the villagers who hunted it down with spears and axes. But the leopard that sometimes prowls round the village at night looking for a stray dog or goat, slinks away at the approach of a human.

I do not see the leopard, but at night, I am woken by a rumbling and thumping on the roof. I wake Gajadhar and ask him what is happening.

'It is only a bear,' he says.

'Is it trying to get in?'

'No, it's been in the cornfield and now it's after the pumpkins on the roof.'

A little later, when we look out of the small window, we see a black bear making off like a thief in the night, a large pumpkin held securely to his chest.

At the approach of winter when snow covers the higher mountains, the brown and black Himalayan bears descend to lower altitudes in search of food. Because they are short-sighted and suspicious of anything that moves, they can be dangerous; but, like most wild animals, they will avoid men if they can and are aggressive only when accompanied by their cubs.

Gajadhar advises me to run downhill if chased by a bear. He says that bears find it easier to run uphill than downhill.

I am not interested in being chased by a bear, but the following night Gajadhar and I stay up to try and prevent the bear from depleting his cornfield. We take up our position on a highway promontory of rock, which gives us a clear view of the moonlit field.

A little after midnight, the bear comes down to the edge of the field but he is suspicious and has probably smelt us. He is, however, hungry; and so, after standing up as high as possible on his hind legs and peering about to see if the field is empty, he comes cautiously out of the forest and makes his way towards the corn.

When about halfway, his attention is suddenly attracted by some Buddhist prayer flags which have been strung up recently between two small trees by a band of wandering Tibetans. On spotting the flags the bear gives a little grunt of disapproval and begins to move back into the forest; but the fluttering of the little flags is a puzzle that he feels he must make out (for a bear is one of the most inquisitive animals); so after a few backward steps, he again stops and watches them.

Not satisfied with this, he stands on his hind legs looking at the flags, first at one side and then at the other. Then seeing that they do not attack him and so not appear dangerous, he makes his way right up to the flags taking only two or three steps at a time and having a good look before each advance. Eventually, he moves confidently up to the flags and pulls them all down. Then, after careful examination of the flags, he moves into the field of corn.

But Gajadhar has decided that he is not going to lose any more corn, so he starts shouting, and the rest of the village wakes up and people come out of their houses beating drums and empty kerosene tins.

Deprived of his dinner, the bear makes off in a bad temper. He runs downhill and at a good speed too; and I am glad that I am not in his path just then. Uphill or downhill, an angry bear is best given a very wide berth.

For Gajadhar, impatient to know the result of his array

entrance examination, the following day is a trial of his patience.

First, we hear that there has been a landslide and that the postman cannot reach us. Then, we hear that although there has been a landslide, the postman has already passed the spot in safety. Another alarming rumour has it that the postman disappeared with the landslide. This is soon denied. The postman is safe. It was only the mailbag that disappeared.

And then, at two in the afternoon, the postman turns up. He tells us that there was indeed a landslide but that it took place on someone else's route. Apparently, a mischievous urchin who passed him on the way was responsible for all the rumours. But we suspect the postman of having something to do with them...

Gajadhar had passed his examination and will leave with me in the morning. We have to be up early in order to reach Lansdowne before dark. But Gajadhar's mother insists on celebrating her son's success by feasting her friends and neighbours. There is a partridge (a present from a neighbour who had decided that Gajadhar will make a fine husband for his daughter), and two chickens: rich fare for folk whose normal diet consists mostly of lentils, potatoes and onions.

After dinner, there are songs, and Gajadhar's mother sings of the homesickness of those who are separated from their loved ones and their home in the hills. It is an old Garhwali folk-song:

Oh, mountain-swift, you are from my father's home;
Speak, oh speak, in the courtyard of my parents,
My mother will hear you; She will send my brother to
fetch me.
A grain of rice alone in the cooking pot
Cries, 'I wish I could get out!'
Likewise I wonder:
'Will I ever reach my father's house?'

The hookah is passed round and stories are told. Tales of ghosts and demons mingle with legends of ancient kings and heroes. It is almost midnight by the time the last guest has gone. Chakradhar approaches me as I am about to retire for the night.

'Will you come again?' he asks.

'Yes, I'll come again,' I reply. 'If not next year, then the year after. How many years are left before you finish school?'

'Four'.

'Four years. If you walk ten miles a day for four years, how many miles will that make?'

'Four thousand and six hundred miles,' says Chakradhar after a moment's thought, 'but we have two months' holiday each year. That means I'll walk about twelve thousand miles in four years.'

The moon has not yet risen. Lanterns swing in the dark.

The lanterns flit silently over the hillside and go out one by one. This Garhwali day, which is just like any other day in the hills, slips quietly into the silence of the mountains.

I stretch myself out on my cot. Outside the small window the sky is brilliant with stars. As I close my eyes, someone brushes against the lime tree, brushing its leaves; and the fresh fragrance of lines comes to me on the night air, making the moment memorable for all time.

A SONG OF MANY RIVERS

1
Suswa River

When I look down from the heights of Landour to the broad Valley of the Doon far below, I can see the little Suswa river, silver in the setting sun, meandering through fields and forests on its way to its confluence with the Ganga.

The Suswa is a river I knew well as a boy, but it has been many years since I took a dip in its quiet pools or rested in the shade of the tall spreading trees growing on its banks. Now I see it from my windows, far away, dreamlike in the mist, and I keep promising myself that I will visit it again, to touch its waters, cool and clear, and feel its rounded pebbles beneath my feet.

It's a little river, flowing down from the ancient Siwaliks and running the length of the valley until, with its sister river the Song, it slips into the Ganga just above the holy city of Haridwar. I could wade across (except during the monsoon when it was in spate) and the water seldom rose above the waist except in sheltered pools, where there were shoals of small fish.

There is a little known and charming legend about the Suswa and its origins, which I have always treasured. It tells us that the Hindu sage, Kasyapa, once gave a great feast to which all the gods were invited. Now Indra, the god of rain, while on his way to the entertainment, happened to meet 60,000 'balkhils' (pygmies) of the Brahmin caste, who were trying in vain to cross a cow's footprint filled with water—to them, a vast lake!

The god could not restrain his amusement. Peals of thunderous laughter echoed across the hills. The indignant Brahmins, determined to have their revenge, at once set to work creating a second Indra, who should supplant the reigning god. This could only be clone by means of penance, fasting and self-denial, in which they persevered until the sweat flowing from their tiny bodies created the 'Suswa' or 'flowing waters' of the little river.

Indra, alarmed at the effect of these religious exercises, sought the help of Brahma, the creator, who taking on the role of a referee, interceded with the priests. Indra was able to keep his position as the rain god.

I saw no pygmies or fairies near the Suswa, but I did see many spotted deer, cheetal, coming down to the water's edge to drink. They are still plentiful in that area.

2

The Nautch Girl's Curse

At the other end of the Doon, far to the west, the Yamuna comes down from the mountains and forms the boundary between the states of Himachal and Uttaranchal. Today, there's a bridge across the river, but many years ago, when I first went across, it was by means of a small cable car, and a very rickety one at that.

During the monsoon, when the river was in spate, the only way across the swollen river was by means of this swaying trolley, which was suspended by a steel rope to two shaky wooden platforms on either bank. There followed a tedious bus journey, during which some sixty-odd miles were covered in six hours. And then you were at Nahan, a small town a little over 3,000 feet above sea level, set amid hill slopes thick with sal and shisham trees. This charming old town links the subtropical Siwaliks to the first foothills of the Himalayas, a unique situation.

The road from Dagshai and Shimla runs into Nahan from the north. No matter in which direction you look, the view is a fine one. To the south stretches the grand panorama of the plains of Saharanpur and Ambala, fronted by two low ranges of thickly forested hills. In the valley below, the pretty Markanda river winds its way out of the Kadir valley.

Nahan's main street is curved and narrow, but well-made and paved with good stone. To the left of the town is the former Raja's palace. Nahan was once the capital of the state of Sirmur, now part of Himachal Pradesh. The original palace was built some three or four hundred years ago, but has been added to from time to time, and is now a large collection of buildings mostly in the Venetian style.

I suppose Nahan qualifies as a hill station, although it can be quite hot in summer. But unlike most hill stations, which are less than two hundred years old, Nahan is steeped in legend and history.

The old capital of Sirmur was destroyed by an earthquake some seven to eight hundred years ago. It was situated some twenty-four miles from present day Nahan, on the west bank of the Giri, where the river expands into a lake. The ancient capital was totally destroyed, with all its inhabitants, and apparently no record was left of its then ruling family. Little remained of the ancient city, just a ruined temple and a few broken stone figures.

As to the cause of the tragedy, the traditional story is that a nautch girl happened to visit Sirmur and performed some wonderful feats. The Raja challenged the girl to walk safely over the Giri on a rope, offering her half his kingdom if she was successful.

The girl accepted the challenge. A rope was stretched across the river. But before starting out, the girl promised that if she fell victim to any treachery on the part of the Raja, a curse would fall upon the city and it would be destroyed by a terrible catastrophe.

While she was on her way to successfully carrying out the feat, some of the Raja's people cut the rope. She fell into the river and was drowned. As predicted, total destruction came to the town.

The founder of the next line of the Sirmur Raja came from the Jaisalmer family in Rajasthan. He was on a pilgrimage to Haridwar with his wife when he heard of the catastrophe that had immolated every member of the state's ancient dynasty. He went at once with his wife into the territory, and established a Jaisalmer Raj. The descent from the first Rajput ruler of Jaisalmer stock, some seven hundred years ago, followed from father to son in an unbroken line. And after much intitial moving about, Nahan was fixed upon as the capital.

The territory was captured by the Gurkhas in 1803, but twelve years later they were expelled by the British after some severe fighting, to which a small English cemetery bears witness. The territory was restored to the Raja, with the exception of the Jaunsar-Bawar region.

Six or seven miles north of Nahan lies the mountain of Jaitak, where the Gurkhas made their last desperate stand. The place is worth a visit, not only for seeing the remains of the Gurkha fort, but also for the magnificent view the mountain commands.

From the northernmost of the mountain's twin peaks, the whole south face of the Himalayas may be seen. From west to north you see the rugged prominences of the Jaunsar Bawar, flanked by the Mussoorie range of hills. It is wild mountain scenery, with a few patches of cultivation and little villages nestling on the sides of the hills. Garhwal and Dehradun are to the cast, and as you go downhill you can see the broad sweep of the Yamuna as it cuts its way through the western Siwaliks.

3

Gently Flows the Ganga

The Bhagirathi is a beautiful river, gentle and caressing (as compared to the turbulent Alaknanda), and pilgrims and others have responded to it with love and respect. The god Shiva released the waters of Goddess Ganga from his locks, and she sped towards the plains in the tracks of Prince Bhagirath's chariot.

> *He held the river on his head*
> *And kept her wandering, where*
> *Dense as Himalaya's woods were spread*
> *The tangles of his hair.*

Revered by Hindus and loved by all, Goddess Ganga weaves her spell over all who come to her. Some assert that the true Ganga (in its upper reaches) is the Alaknanda. Geographically, this may be so. But tradition carries greater weight in the abode of the Gods, and traditionally the Bhagirathi is the Ganga. Of course, the two rivers meet at Devprayag, in the foothills, and this marriage of the waters settles the issue.

I put the question to my friend Dr Sudhakar Misra, from whom words of wisdom sometimes flow; and true to form, he answered: 'The Alaknanda is Ganga, but the Bhagirathi is Ganga-ji.'

She issues from the very heart of the Himalayas. Visiting

Gangotri in 1820, the writer and traveller Baillie Fraser noted: 'We are now in the centre of the Himalayas, the loftiest and perhaps the most rugged range of mountains in the world.'

Here, at the source of the river, we come to the realization that we are at the very centre and heart of things. One has an almost primaeval sense of belonging to these mountains and to this valley in particular. For me, and for many who have been here, the Bhagirathi is the most beautiful of the four main river valleys of Garhwal.

The Bhagirathi seems to have everything—a gentle disposition, deep glens and forests, the ultravision of an open valley graced with tiers of cultivation leading up by degrees to the peaks and glaciers at its head.

At Tehri, the big dam slows down Prince Bhagirath's chariot. But upstream, from Bhatwari to Harsil, there are extensive pine forests. They fill the ravines and plateaus, before giving way to yew and cypress, oak and chestnut. Above 9,000 feet the deodar (*devdar*, tree of the gods) is the principal tree. It grows to a little distance above Gangotri, and then gives way to the birch, which is found in patches to within half a mile of the glacier.

It was the valuable timber of the deodar that attracted the adventurer Frederick 'Pahari' Wilson to the valley in the 1850s. He leased the forests from the Raja of Tehri, and within a few years he had made a fortune. From his horse and depot at Harsil, he would float the logs downstream to Tehri, where they would be sawn up and despatched to buyers in the cities.

Bridge-building was another of Wilson's ventures. The most famous of these was a 350 feet suspension bridge at Bhaironghat, over 1,200 feet above the young Bhagirathi where it thunders through a deep defile. This rippling contraption was at first a source of terror to travellers, and only a few ventured across it.

To reassure people, Wilson would mount his horse and gallop to and fro across the bridge. It has since collapsed, but local people will tell you that the ghostly hoof beats of Wilson's horse can still be heard on full moon nights. The supports of the old bridge were massive deodar trunks, and they can still be seen to one side of the new road bridge built by engineers of the Northern Railway.

The old forest rest houses at Dharasu, Bhatwari and Harsil were all built by Wilson as staging posts, for the only roads were narrow tracks linking one village to another. Wilson married a local girl, Gulabi, from the village of Mukhba, and the portraits of the Wilsons (early examples of the photographer's art) still hang in these sturdy little bungalows. At any rate, I found their pictures at Bhatwari. Harsil is now out of bounds to civilians, and I believe, part of the old house was destroyed in a fire a few years ago. This sturdy building withstood the earthquake which devastated the area in 1991.

Amongst other things, Wilson introduced the apple into this area, 'Wilson apples'—large, red and juicy—sold to travellers and pilgrims on their way to Gangotri. This fascinating man also acquired an encyclopaedic knowledge of the wildlife of the region, and his articles, which appeared in *Indian Sporting Life* in the 1860s, were later plundered by so-called wildlife writers for their own works.

He acquired properties in Dehradun and Mussoorie, and his wife lived there in some style, giving him three sons. Two died young. The third, Charlie Wilson, went through most of his father's fortune. His grave lies next to my grandfather's grave in the old Dehradun cemetery. Gulabi is buried in Mussoorie, next to her husband. I wrote this haiku for her:

Her beauty brought her fame,
But only the wild rose growing beside her grave
Is there to hear her whispered name—
Gulabi.

I remember old Mrs Wilson, Charlie's widow, when I was a boy in Dehra. She lived next door in what was the last of the Wilson properties. Her nephew, Geoffrey Davis, went to school with me in Shimla, and later joined the Indian Air Force. But luck never went the way of Wilson's descendants, and Geoffrey died when his plane crashed.

Wilson's life is a fit subject for a romance; but even if one were never written, his legend would live on, as it has done for over a hundred years. There has never been any attempt to commemorate him, but people in the valley still speak of him in awe and admiration, as though he had lived only yesterday.

Some men leave a trail of legend behind them because they give their spirit to the place where they have lived, and remain forever a part of the rocks and mountain streams.

Gangotri is situated at just a little over 10,300 feet. On the right bank of the river is the Gangotri temple, a small neat building without too much ornamentation, built by Amar Singh Thapa, a Nepali General, early in the nineteenth century. It was renovated by the Maharaja of Jaipur in the 1920s. The rock on which it stands is called Bhagirath Shila and is said to be the place where Prince Bhagirath did penance in order that Ganga be brought down from her abode of eternal snow. Here the rocks are carved and polished by ice and water, so smooth that in places they look like rolls of silk. The fast-flowing waters of this mountain torrent look very different from the huge sluggish river that finally empties its waters into the Bay of Bengal fifteen hundred miles away.

The river emerges from beneath a great glacier, thickly studded with enormous loose rocks and earth. The glacier is about a mile in width and extends upwards for many miles. The chasm in the glacier through which the stream rushed forth into the light of day is named Gaumukh, the cow's mouth, and is held in deepest reverence by Hindus. The regions of eternal frost in the vicinity were the scene of many of their most sacred mysteries.

The Ganga enters the world no puny stream, but bursts from its icy womb a river thirty or forty yards in breadth. At Gauri Kund (below the Gangotri temple) it falls over a rock of considerable height and continues tumbling over a succession of small cascades until it enters the Bhaironghati gorge.

A night spent beside the river, within the sound of the fall, is an eerie experience. After some time it begins to sound, not like one fall but a hundred, and this sound permeates both one's dreams and waking hours. Rising early to greet the dawn proved rather pointless at Gangotri, for the surrounding peaks did not let the sun in till after 9 a.m. Everyone rushed about to keep warm, exclaiming delightedly at what they call 'gulabi thand', literally, 'rosy cold'. Guaranteed to turn the cheeks a rosy pink! A charming expression, but I prefer a rosy sunburn, and remained beneath a heavy quilt until the sun came up to throw its golden shafts across the river.

This is mid-October, and after Diwali the shrine and the small township will close for winter, the pandits retreating to the relative warmth of Mukbha. Soon snow will cover everything, and even the hardy purple-plumaged whistling thrushes, lovers of deep shade, will move further down the valley. And down below the forest-line, the Garhwali farmers go about harvesting their terraced fields which form patterns of yellow, green and gold above the deep green of the river.

Yes, the Bhagirathi is a green river. Although deep and swift, it does not lose its serenity. At no place does it look hurried or confused—unlike the turbulent Alaknanda, fretting and frothing as it goes crashing down its boulder-strewn bed. The Alaknanda gives one a feeling of being trapped, because the river itself is trapped. The Bhagirathi is free-flowing, easy. At all times and places it seems to find its true level.

In the old days, only the staunchest of pilgrims visited the shrines at Gangotri and Jamnotri. The roads were rocky and dangerous, winding along in some places, ascending and descending the faces of deep precipices and ravines, at times leading along banks of loose earth where landslides had swept the original path away.

There are still no large towns above Uttarkashi, and this absence of large centres of population may be reason why the forests are better preserved than those in the Alaknanda valley, or further downstream. Uttarkashi, though a large and growing town, is as yet uncrowded. The seediness of towns like Rishikesh and parts of Dehradun is not yet evident here. One can take a leisurely walk through its long (and well-supplied) bazaar, without being jostled by crowds or knocked over by three-wheelers. Here, too, the river is always with you, and you must live in harmony with its sound as it goes rushing and humming along its shingly bed.

Uttarkashi is not without its own religious and historical importance, although all traces of its ancient town of Barahat appear to have vanished. There are four important temples here, and on the occasion of Makar Sankranti, early in January a week-long fair is held when thousands from the surrounding areas throng the roads to the town. To the beating of drums and blowing of trumpets, the gods and goddesses are brought to the fair in gaily decorated palanquins. The surrounding villages wear a deserted look that day as everyone flocks to the temples and bathing ghats and to the entertainments of the fair itself.

We have to move far downstream to reach another large centre of population, the town of Tehri, and this is a very different place from Uttarkashi. Tehri has all the characteristics of a small town in the plains—crowds, noise, traffic congestion, dust and refuse, scruffy dhabas—with this difference that here it is all ephemeral, for Tehri is destined to be submerged by the water of the Bhagirathi when the Tehri dam is finally completed.

The rulers of Garhwal were often changing their capitals, and when, after the Gurkha War (of 1811–15), the former capital of Srinagar became part of British Garhwal, Raja Sudershan Shah established his new capital at Tehri. It is said that when he reached this spot, his horse refused to go any further. This was enough for the king, it seems; or so the story goes.

Perhaps Prince Bhagirath's chariot will come to a halt here too, when the dam is built. The two hundred and forty-six metre high earthen dam, with forty-two square miles of reservoir capacity, will submerge the town and about thirty villages.

But as we leave the town and cross the narrow bridge over the river, a mighty blast from above sends rocks hurtling down the defile, just to remind us that work is indeed in progress.

Unlike the Raja's horse, I have no wish to be stopped in my tracks at Tehri. There are livelier places upstream. And as for Ganga herself, that deceptively gentle river, I wonder if she will take kindly to our efforts to contain her.

4

Falling for Mandakini

A great river at its confluence with another great river is, for me, a special moment in time. And so it was with the

Mandakini at Rudraprayag, where its waters joined the waters of the Alaknanda, the one having come from the glacial snows above Kedarnath, the other from the Himalayan heights beyond Badrinath. Both sacred rivers, destined to become the holy Ganga further downstream.

I fell in love with the Mandakini at first sight. Or was it the valley that I fell in love with? I am not sure, and it doesn't really matter. The valley is the river.

While the Alaknanda valley, especially in its higher reaches, is a deep and narrow gorge where precipitous outcrops of rock hang threateningly over the traveller, the Mandakini valley is broader, gentler, the terraced fields wider, the banks of the river a green sward in many places. Somehow, one does not feel that one is at the mercy of the Mandakini whereas one is always at the mercy of the Alaknanda with its sudden floods.

Rudraprayag is hot. It is probably a pleasant spot in winter, but at the end of June, it is decidedly hot. Perhaps its chief claim to fame is that it gave its name to the dreaded man-eating leopard of Rudraprayag, who in the course of seven years (1918–25) accounted for more than 300 victims. It was finally shot by Jim Corbett, who recounted the saga of his long hunt for the killer in his fine book, *The Man-eating Leopard of Rudraprayag.*

The place at which the leopard was shot was the village of Gulabrai, two miles south of Rudraprayag. Under a large mango tree stands a memorial raised to Jim Corbett by officers and men of the Border Roads Organisation. It is a touching gesture to one who loved Garhwal and India. Unfortunately, several buffaloes are tethered close by, and one has to wade through slush and buffalo dung to get to the memorial stone. A board tacked on to the mango tree attracts the attention of motorists who might pass without noticing the memorial, which is off to one side.

The killer leopard was noted for its direct method of attack on humans; and, in spite of being poisoned, trapped in a cave, and shot at innumerable times, it did not lose its contempt for man. Two English sportsmen covering both ends to the old suspension bridge over the Alaknanda fired several times at the man-eater but to little effect.

It was not long before the leopard acquired a reputation among the hill folk for being an evil spirit. A sadhu was suspected of turning into the leopard by night, and was only saved from being lynched by the ingenuity of Philip Mason, then deputy commissioner of Garhwal. Mason kept the sadhu in custody until the leopard made his next attack, thus proving the man innocent. Years later, when Mason turned novelist and (using the pen name Philip Woodruffe) wrote *The Wild Sweet Witch,* he had one of the characters, a beautiful young woman who apparently turns into a man-eating leopard by night.

Corbett's host at Gulabrai was one of the few who survived an encounter with the leopard. It left him with a hole in his throat. Apart from being a superb storyteller, Corbett displayed great compassion for people from all walks of life and is still a legend in Garhwal and Kumaon amongst people who have never read his books.

In June, one does not linger long in the steamy heat of Rudraprayag. But as one travels up the river, making a gradual ascent of the Mandakini valley, there is a cool breeze coming down from the snows, and the smell of rain is in the air.

The thriving little township of Agastmuni spreads itself along the wide riverbanks. Further upstream, near a little place called Chandrapuri, we cannot resist breaking our journey to sprawl on the tender green grass that slopes gently down to the swift-flowing river. A small rest house is in the making. Around it, banana fronds sway and poplar leaves dance in the breeze.

This is no sluggish river of the plains, but a fast moving

current, tumbling over rocks, turning and twisting in its efforts to discover the easiest way for its frothy snow-fed waters to escape the mountains. Escape is the word! For the constant plaint of many a Garliwali is that, while his hills abound in rivers, the water runs down and away, and little if any reaches the fields and villages above it. Cultivation must depend on the rain and not on the river.

The road climbs gradually, still keeping to the river. Just outside Guptakashi, my attention is drawn to a clump of huge trees sheltering a small but ancient temple. We stop here and enter the shade of the trees.

The temple is deserted. It is a temple dedicated to Shiva, and in the courtyard are several river-rounded stone *lingarns* on which leaves and blossoms have fallen. No one seems to come here, which is strange, since it is on the pilgrim route. Two boys from a neighbouring field leave their yoked bullock to come and talk to me, but they cannot tell me much about the temple except to confirm that it is seldom visited. 'The buses do not stop here.' That seems explanation enough. For where the buses go, the pilgrims go; and where the pilgrims go, other pilgrims will follow. Thus far and no further.

The trees seem to be magnolias. But I have never seen magnolia trees grow to such huge proportions. Perhaps they are something else. Never mind; let them remain a mystery.

Guptakashi in the evening is all a bustle. A coachload of pilgrims (headed for Kedarnath) has just arrived, and the tea shops near the bus stand are doing brisk business. Then the 'local' bus from Ukhimath, across the river arrives, and many of the passengers head for a tea shop famed for its *samosas*. The local bus is called the *Bhook Hartal,* the 'Hunger-Strike' bus.

'How did it get that name?' I asked one of the samosa eaters.

'Well, it's an interesting story. For a long time we had

been asking the authorities to provide a bus service for the local people and for the villagers who live off the roads. All the buses came from Srinagar or Rishikesh, and were taken up by pilgrims. The locals couldn't find room in them. But our pleas went unheard until the whole town, or most of it, decided to go on hunger strike.'

'They nearly put me out of business too,' said the tea shop owner cheerfully. 'Nobody ate any samosas for two days!'

There is no cinema or public place of entertainment at Guptakashi, and the town goes to sleep early. And wakes early.

At six, the hillside, green from recent rain, sparkles in the morning sunshine. Snow-capped Chaukhamba (7,140 metres) is dazzling. The air is clear; no smoke or dust up here. The climate, I am told, is mild all year round judging by the scent and shape of the flowers, and the boys call them Champs, Hindi for champa blossom. Ukhimath, on the other side of the river, lies in the shadow. It gets the sun at nine. In winter, it must wait till afternoon.

Guptakashi has not yet been rendered ugly by the barrack-type architecture that has come up in some growing hill towns. The old double-storeyed houses are built of stone, with gray slate roofs. They blend well with the hillside. Cobbled paths meander through the old bazaar.

One of these takes up to the famed Guptakashi temple, tucked away above the old part of the town. Here, as in Benaras, Shiva is worshipped as Vishwanath, and two underground streams representing the sacred Jamuna and Bhagirathi rivers feed the pool sacred to the God. This temple gives the town its name, Gupta-Kashi, the 'Invisible Benaras', just as Uttarkashi on the Bhagirathi is 'Upper Benaras'.

Guptakashi and its environs have so many *linganis* that the saying *June Kanhar Utne Shanhar*—'As many stones, so many

Shivas'—has become a proverb to describe its holiness.

From Guptakashi, pilgrims proceed north to Kedarnath, and the last stage of their journey—about a day's march—must be covered on foot or horseback. The temple of Kedarnath, situated at a height of 11,753 feet, is encircled by snow-capped peaks, and Atkinson has conjectured that 'the symbol of the *linga* may have arisen front the pointed peaks around his (God Shiva's) original home.'

The temple is dedicated to Sadashiva, the subterranean form of the God, who, 'fleeing from the Pandavas took refuge here in the form of a he-buffalo and finding himself hard- pressed, dived into the ground leaving the hinder parts on the surface, which continue to be the subject of adoration.' (Atkinson)

The other portions of the God are worshipped as follows: the arms at Tunguath, at a height of 13,000 feet, the face at Rudranath (12,000 feet), the belly at Madmaheshwar, 18 miles northeast of Guptakashi; and the hair and head at Kalpeshwar, near Joshimath. These five sacred shrines form the *Panch Kedar* (five Kedars).

We leave the Mandakini to visit Tungnath on the Chandrashila range. But I will return to this river. It has captured my mind and heart.

RUNNING FOR COVER

The right to privacy is a fine concept and might actually work in the West, but in Eastern lands it is purely notional. If I want to be left alone, I have to be a shameless liar—pretend that I am out of town or, if that doesn't work, announce that I have measles, mumps or some new variety of Asian flu.

Now I happen to like people and I like meeting people from all walks of life. If this were not the case, I would have nothing to write about. But I don't like too many people all at once. They tend to get in the way. And if they arrive without warning, banging on my door while I am in the middle of composing a poem or writing a story, or simply enjoying my afternoon siesta, I am inclined to be snappy or unwelcoming. Occasionally I have even turned people away.

As I get older, that afternoon siesta becomes more of a necessity and less of an indulgence. But it's strange how people love to call on me between two and four in the afternoon. I suppose it's the time of day when they have nothing to do.

'How do we get through the afternoon?' one of them will say.

'I know! Let's go and see old Ruskin. He's sure to entertain us with some stimulating conversation, if nothing else.' Stimulating conversation in mid-afternoon? Even Socrates would have balked at it.

'I'm sorry I can't see you today,' I mutter. 'I don't feel at all well.' (In fact, extremely unwell at the prospect of several strangers gaping at me for at least half-an-hour.)

'Not well? We're so sorry. My wife here is a homeopath.'

It's amazing the number of homeopaths who turn up at my door. Unfortunately they never seem to have their little powders on them, those miracle cures for everything from headaches to hernias.

The other day a family burst in—uninvited of course. The husband was an ayurvedic physician, the wife was a homeopath (naturally), the eldest boy a medical student at an allopathic medical college.

'What do you do when one of you falls ill?' I asked, 'Do you try all three systems of medicine?'

'It depends on the ailment,' said the young man. 'But we seldom fall ill. My sister here is a yoga expert.'

His sister, a hefty girl in her late twenties (still single) looked more like an all-in wrestler than a supple yoga practitioner. She looked at my tummy. She could see I was in bad shape.

'I could teach you some exercises,' she said. 'But you'd have to come to Ludhiana.'

I felt grateful that Ludhiana was a six-hour drive from Mussoorie.

'I'll drop in some day,' I said. 'In fact, I'll come and take a course.'

We parted on excellent terms. But it doesn't always turn out that way.

There was this woman, very persistent, in fact downright rude, who wouldn't go away even when I told her I had bird-flu.

'I have to see you,' she said, 'I've written a novel, and I want you to recommend it for the Booker Prize.'

'I'm afraid I have no influence there,' I pleaded. 'I'm completely unknown in Britain.'

'Then how about the Nobel Prize?'

I thought about that for a minute. 'Only in the science field,' I said. 'If it's something to do with genes or stem cells?'

She looked at me as though I was some kind of worm. 'You are not very helpful,' she said.

'Well, let me read your book.'

'I haven't written it yet.'

'Well, why not come back when it's finished? Give yourself a year—two years—these things should never be done in a hurry.' I guided her to the gate and encouraged her down the steps.

'You are very rude,' she said. 'You did not even ask me in. I'll report you to Khushwant Singh. He's a friend of mine. He'll put you in his column.'

'If Khushwant Singh is your friend,' I said, 'why are you bothering with me? He knows all the Nobel and Booker Prize people. All the important people, in fact.'

I did not see her again, but she got my phone number from someone, and now she rings me once a week to tell me her book is coming along fine. Any day now, she's going to turn up with the manuscript.

Casual visitors who bring me their books or manuscripts are the ones I dread most. They ask me for an opinion, and if I give them a frank assessment they resent it. It's unwise to tell a would-be writer that his memoirs or novel or collected verse would be better off unpublished. Murders have been committed for less. So I play safe and say, 'Very promising. Carry on writing.' But this is fatal. Almost immediately I am asked to write a foreword or introduction, together with a letter of recommendation to my publisher—or any publisher of standing. Unwillingly I become a literacy agent; unpaid of course.

I am all for encouraging the arts and literature, but I do think writers should seek out their own publishers and write their own introductions.

The perils of doing this sort of thing was illustrated when 1 was prevailed upon to write a short introduction to a book about a dreaded man-eater who had taken a liking to the flesh of the good people of Dogadda, near Lansdowne. The author of the book could hardly write a decent sentence, but he managed to string together a lengthy account of the leopard's depredations. He was so persistent, calling on me or ringing me up that I finally did the introduction. He then wanted me to edit or touch up his manuscript; but this I refused to do. I would starve if I had to sit down and rewrite other people's books. But he prevailed upon me to give him a photograph.

Months later, the book appeared, printed privately of course. And there was my photograph, and a photograph of the dead leopard after it had been hunted down. But the local printer had got the captions mixed up. The dead animal's picture earned the line: 'Well-known author Ruskin Bond.' My picture carried the legend: 'Dreaded man-eater, shot after it had killed its 26th victim.'

The printer's devil had turned me into a serial killer.

Now you know why I'm wary of writing introductions.

'Vanity' publishers thrive on writers who are desperate to see their work in print. They will print and deliver a book at your doorstep and then leave you with the task of selling it; or to be more accurate, disposing of it.

One of my neighbours, Mrs Santra—may her soul rest in peace—paid a publisher forty-thousand rupees to bring out a fancy edition of her late husband's memoirs. During his lifetime, he'd been unable to get it published, but before he died he got his wife to promise that she'd publish it for him. This she did, and the publisher duly delivered 500 copies to the good lady. She gave a few copies to friends, and then passed away, leaving the books behind. Her heir is now saddled with 450 hardbound volumes of unsaleable memoirs.

I have always believed that if a writer is any good he will find a publisher who will print, bind, and sell his books, and even give him a royalty for his efforts. A writer who pays to get published is inviting disappointment and heartbreak.

Many people are under the impression that I live in splendour in a large mansion, surrounded by secretaries and servants. They are disappointed to find that I live in a tiny bedroom-cum-study and that my living room is so full of books that there is hardly space for more than three or four visitors at a time.

Sometimes thirty to forty schoolchildren turn up, wanting to see me. I don't turn away children, if I can help it. But if they come in large numbers I have to meet and talk to them on the road, which is inconvenient for everyone.

If I had the means, would I live in a splendid mansion in the more affluent parts of Mussoorie, with a film star or TV personality as my neighbour? I rather doubt it. All my life I've been living in one or two rooms and I don't think I could manage a bigger establishment. True, my extended family takes up another two rooms, but they see to it that my working space is not violated. And if I am hard at work (or fast asleep) they will try to protect me from unheralded or unwelcome visitors.

And I have learnt to tell lies. Especially when I'm asked to attend school functions as a chief guest or in some formal capacity. To spend two or three hours listening to speeches (and then being expected to give one) is my idea of hell. It's hell for the students and it's hell for me. The speeches are usually followed (or preceded) by folk dances, musical interludes or class plays, and this only adds to the torment. Sports days are just as bad. You can skip the speeches (hopefully), but you must sit out in the hot sun for the greater part of the day, while a loudspeaker informs you that little Parshottam has just broken the school record for the under-nine high jump, or that Pamela Highjinks has won the hurdles for the third year running. You don't get to see the events because you are kept busy making polite conversation with the other guests. The only occasion when a sports event really came to life was when a misdirected discus narrowly missed decapitating the headmaster's wife.

Former athletes and sportsmen seldom visit me. They have difficulty making it up my steps. Most of them have problems with their knees before they are fifty. They hobble (for want of a better word). Once their playing days are over, they start hobbling. Nandu, a former tennis champion, can't make it up my steps, nor can Chand—a former wrestler. Too much physical activity when young has resulted in an early breakdown of the body's machinery. As Nandu says, 'Body can't take it any more.' I'm not too agile either, but then, I was never much of a sportsman. Second last in the marathon was probably my most memorable achievement.

Oddly enough, some of the most frequent visitors to my humble abode are honeymooners.

Why, I don't know, but they always ask for my blessing even though I am hardly an advertisement for married bliss. A seventy-year-old bachelor blessing a newly married couple? Maybe they are under the impression that I'm a Brahmachari? But how would that help them? They are going to have babies sooner or later.

It is seldom that they happen to be readers or book lovers, so why pick an author, and that too one who does not go to places of worship? However, since these young couples are inevitably attractive, and full of high hopes for their future and the future of mankind, I am happy to talk to them, wish them well...and if it's a blessing they want, they are welcome. My hands are far from being saintly but at least they are well-intentioned.

I have, at times, been mistaken for other people.

'Are you Mr Pickwick?' asked a small boy. At least he'd been reading Dickens. A distant relative, I said, and beamed at him in my best Pickwickian manner.

I am at ease with children, who talk quite freely except when accompanied by their parents. Then it's mum and dad who do all the talking.

'My son studies your book in school,' said one fond mother, proudly exhibiting her ten-year-old. 'He wants your autograph.'

'What's the name of the book you're reading?' I asked.

'Tom Sawyer,' he said promptly.

So I signed Mark Twain in his autograph book. He seemed quite happy.

A schoolgirl asked me to autograph her maths textbook.

'But I failed in maths,' I said. 'I'm just a story writer.'

'How much did you get?'

'Four out of a hundred.'

She looked at me rather crossly and snatched the book away.

I have signed books in the names of Enid Blyton, R.K. Narayan, Ian Botham, Daniel Defoe, Harry Potter and the Swiss Family Robinson. No one seems to mind.

ANGRY RIVER

In the middle of the big river, the river that began in the mountains and ended in the sea, was a small island. The river swept round the island, sometimes clawing at its banks, but never going right over it. It was over twenty years since the river had flooded the island, and at that time no one had lived there. But for the last ten years a small hut had stood there, a mud-walled hut with a sloping thatched roof. The hut had been built into a huge rock, so only three of the walls were mud, and the fourth was rock.

Goats grazed on the short grass which grew on the island, and on the prickly leaves of thorn bushes. A few hens followed them about. There was a melon patch and a vegetable patch.

In the middle of the island stood a peepul tree. It was the only tree there.

Even during the Great Flood, when the island had been under water, the tree had stood firm.

It was an old tree. A seed had been carried to the island by a strong wind some fifty years back, had found shelter between two rocks, had taken root there, and had sprung up to give shade and shelter to a small family; and Indians love peepul trees, especially during the hot summer months when the heart-shaped leaves catch the least breath of air and flutter eagerly, fanning those who sit beneath.

A sacred tree, the peepul: the abode of spirits, good and bad.

'Don't yawn when you are sitting beneath the tree,' Grandmother used to warn Sita. 'And if you must yawn, always snap your fingers in front of your mouth. If you forget to do that, a spirit might jump down your throat!'

'And then what will happen?' asked Sita.

'It will probably ruin your digestion,' said Grandfather, who wasn't much of a believer in spirits.

The peepul had a beautiful leaf, and Grandmother likened it to the body of the mighty god Krishna—broad at the shoulders, then tapering down to a very slim waist.

It was an old tree, and an old man sat beneath it.

He was mending a fishing net. He had fished in the river for ten years, and he was a good fisherman. He knew where to find the slim silver Chilwa fish and the big beautiful Mahseer and the long-moustached Singhara; he knew where the river was deep and where it was shallow; he knew which baits to use— which fish liked worms and which liked gram. He had taught his son to fish, but his son had gone to work in a factory in a city, nearly a hundred miles away. He had no grandson; but he had a granddaughter, Sita, and she could do all the things a boy could do, and sometimes she could do them better. She had lost her mother when she was very small. Grandmother had taught her all the things a girl should know, and she could do these as well as most girls. But neither of her grandparents could read or write, and as a result Sita couldn't read or write either.

There was a school in one of the villages across the river, but Sita had never seen it. There was too much to do on the island.

While Grandfather mended his net, Sita was inside the hut, pressing her Grandmother's forehead, which was hot with fever. Grandmother had been ill for three days and could not eat. She had been ill before, but she had never been so bad. Grandfather had brought her some sweet oranges from the market in the nearest town, and she could suck the juice from the oranges, but she couldn't eat anything else.

She was younger than Grandfather, but because she was sick, she looked much older. She had never been very strong.

When Sita noticed that Grandmother had fallen asleep, she tiptoed out of the room on her bare feet and stood outside.

The sky was dark with monsoon clouds. It had rained all night, and in a few hours it would rain again. The monsoon rains had come early, at the end of June. Now it was the middle of July, and already the river was swollen. Its rushing sound seemed nearer and more menacing than usual.

Sita went to her grandfather and sat down beside him beneath the peepul tree.

'When you are hungry, tell me,' she said, 'and I will make the bread.'

'Is your grandmother asleep?'

'She sleeps. But she will wake soon, for she has a deep pain.'

The old man stared out across the river, at the dark green of the forest, at the grey sky, and said, 'Tomorrow, if she is not better, I will take her to the hospital at Shahganj. There they will know how to make her well. You may be on your own for a few days—but you have been on your own before…'

Sita nodded gravely; she had been alone before, even during the rainy season. Now she wanted Grandmother to get well, and she knew that only Grandfather had the skill to take the small dugout boat across the river when the current was so strong. Someone would have to stay behind to look after their few possessions.

Sita was not afraid of being alone, but she did not like the look of the river. That morning, when she had gone down to fetch water, she had noticed that the level had risen. Those rocks which were normally spattered with the droppings of snipe and curlew and other waterbirds had suddenly disappeared.

They disappeared every year—but not so soon, surely?

'Grandfather, if the river rises, what will I do?'

'You will keep to the high ground.'

'And if the water reaches the high ground?'

'Then take the hens into the hut, and stay there.'

'And if the water comes into the hut?'

'Then climb into the peepul tree. It is a strong tree. It will not fall. And the water cannot rise higher than the tree!'

'And the goats, Grandfather?'

'I will be taking them with me, Sita. I may have to sell them to pay for good food and medicines for your grandmother. As for the hens, if it becomes necessary, put them on the roof. But do not worry too much'—and he patted Sita's head—'the water will not rise as high. I will be back soon, remember that.'

'And won't Grandmother come back?'

'Yes, of course, but they may keep her in the hospital for some time.'

◆

Towards evening, it began to rain again—big pellets of rain, scarring the surface of the river. But it was warm rain, and Sita could move about in it. She was not afraid of getting wet, she rather liked it. In the previous month, when the first monsoon shower had arrived, washing the dusty leaves of the tree and bringing up the good smell of the earth, she had exulted in it, had run about shouting with joy. She was used to it now, and indeed a little tired of the rain, but she did not mind getting wet. It was steamy indoors, and her thin dress would soon dry in the heat from the kitchen fire.

She walked about barefooted, barelegged. She was very sure on her feet; her toes had grown accustomed to gripping all kinds of rocks, slippery or sharp. And though thin, she was surprisingly strong.

Black hair, streaming across her face. Black eyes. Slim brown arms. A scar on her thigh—when she was small, visiting her mother's village, a hyaena had entered the house where she was sleeping, fastened on to her leg and tried to drag her away, but her screams had roused the villagers and the hyaena had run off.

She moved about in the pouring rain, chasing the hens into a shelter behind the hut. A harmless brown snake, flooded out of its hole, was moving across the open ground. Sita picked up a stick, scooped the snake up, and dropped it between a cluster of rocks. She had no quarrel with snakes. They kept down the rats and the frogs. She wondered how the rats had first come to the island—probably in someone's boat, or in a sack of grain. Now it was a job to keep their numbers down.

When Sita finally went indoors, she was hungry. She ate some dried peas and warmed up some goat's milk.

Grandmother woke once and asked for water, and Grandfather held the brass tumbler to her lips.

◆

It rained all night.

The roof was leaking, and a small puddle formed on the floor. They kept the kerosene lamp alight. They did not need the light, but somehow it made them feel safer.

The sound of the river had always been with them, although they were seldom aware of it; but that night they noticed a change in its sound. There was something like a moan, like a wind in the tops of tall trees and a swift hiss as the water swept round the rocks and carried away pebbles. And sometimes there was a rumble, as loose earth fell into the water.

Sita could not sleep.

She had a rag doll, made with Grandmother's help out of bits of old clothing. She kept it by her side every night. The doll was someone to talk to, when the nights were long and sleep elusive. Her grandparents were often ready to talk—and Grandmother, when she was well, was a good storyteller—but sometimes Sita wanted to have secrets, and though there were no special secrets in her life, she made up a few, because it was fun to have them. And if you have secrets, you must have a friend to share them with, a companion of one's own age. Since there were no other children on the island, Sita shared her secrets with the rag doll whose name was Mumta.

Grandfather and Grandmother were asleep, though the sound of Grandmother's laboured breathing was almost as persistent as the sound of the river.

'Mumta,' whispered Sita in the dark, starting one of her private conversations. 'Do you think Grandmother will get well again?'

Mumta always answered Sita's questions, even though the answers could only be heard by Sita.

'She is very old,' said Mumta.

'Do you think the river will reach the hut?' asked Sita.

'If it keeps raining like this, and the river keeps rising, it will reach the hut.'

'I am a little afraid of the river, Mumta. Aren't you afraid?'

'Don't be afraid. The river has always been good to us.'

'What will we do if it comes into the hut?'

'We will climb onto the roof.'

'And if it reaches the roof?'

'We will climb the peepul tree. The river has never gone higher than the peepul tree.'

As soon as the first light showed through the little skylight, Sita got up and went outside. It wasn't raining hard, it was drizzling, but it was the sort of drizzle that could continue for days, and it probably meant that heavy rain was falling in the hills where the river originated.

Sita went down to the water's edge. She couldn't find her favourite rock, the one on which she often sat dangling her feet in the water, watching the little Chilwa fish swim by. It was still there, no doubt, but the river had gone over it.

She stood on the sand, and she could feel the water oozing and bubbling beneath her feet.

The river was no longer green and blue and flecked with white, but a muddy colour.

She went back to the hut. Grandfather was up now. He was getting his boat ready.

Sita milked the goat. Perhaps it was the last time she would milk it.

◆

The sun was just coming up when Grandfather pushed off in the boat. Grandmother lay in the prow. She was staring hard at Sita, trying to speak, but the words would not come. She raised her hand in a blessing.

Sita bent and touched her grandmother's feet, and then Grandfather pushed off. The little boat—with its two old people and three goats—riding swiftly on the river, moved slowly, very slowly, towards the opposite bank. The current was so swift now that Sita realized the boat would be carried about half a mile downstream before Grandfather could get it to dry land.

It bobbed about on the water, getting smaller and smaller, until it was just a speck on the broad river.

And suddenly Sita was alone.

There was a wind, whipping the raindrops against her face; and there was the water, rushing past the island; and there was the distant shore, blurred by rain; and there was the small hut; and there was the tree.

Sita got busy. The hens had to be fed. They weren't bothered about anything except food. Sita threw them handfuls of coarse grain and potato peelings and peanut shells.

Then she took the broom and swept out the hut, lit the charcoal burner, warmed some milk and thought, 'Tomorrow there will be no milk…' She began peeling onions. Soon her eyes started smarting and, pausing for a few moments and glancing round the quiet room, she became aware again that she was alone. Grandfather's hookah pipe stood by itself in one corner. It was a beautiful old hookah, which had belonged to Sita's great-grandfather. The bowl was made out of a coconut encased in silver. The long winding stem was at least four feet in length. It was their most valuable possession. Grandmother's sturdy shisham-wood walking stick stood in another corner.

Sita looked around for Mumta, found the doll beneath the cot, and placed her within sight and hearing.

Thunder rolled down from the hills. BOOM—BOOM—BOOM…

'The gods of the mountains are angry,' said Sita. 'Do you think they are angry with me?'

'Why should they be angry with you?' asked Mumta.

'They don't have to have a reason for being angry. They are angry with everything, and we are in the middle of everything. We are so small—do you think they know we are here?'

'Who knows what the gods think?'

'But I made you,' said Sita, 'and I know you are here.'

'And will you save me if the river rises?'

'Yes, of course. I won't go anywhere without you, Mumta.'

Sita couldn't stay indoors for long. She went out, taking Mumta with her, and stared out across the river to the safe land on the other side. But was it safe there? The river looked much wider now. Yes, it had crept over its banks and spread far across the flat plain. Far away, people were driving their cattle through waterlogged, flooded fields, carrying their belongings in bundles on their heads or shoulders, leaving their homes, making for the high land. It wasn't safe anywhere.

She wondered what had happened to Grandfather and Grandmother. If they had reached the shore safely, Grandfather would have to engage a bullock cart, or a pony-drawn carriage, to get Grandmother to the district town, five or six miles away, where there was a market, a court, a jail, a cinema and a hospital.

She wondered if she would ever see Grandmother again. She had done her best to look after the old lady, remembering the times when Grandmother had looked after her, had gently touched her fevered brow and had told her stories—stories about the gods: about the young Krishna, friend of birds and animals, so full of mischief, always causing confusion among the other gods; and Indra, who made the thunder and lightning; and Vishnu, the preserver of all good things, whose steed was a great white bird; and Ganesh, with the elephant's head; and Hanuman, the monkey-god, who helped the young Prince Rama in his war with the King of Ceylon. Would Grandmother return to tell her more about them, or would she have to find out for herself?

The island looked much smaller now. In parts, the mudbanks had dissolved quickly, sinking into the river. But in the middle of the island there was rocky ground, and the rocks would never crumble, they could only be submerged. In a space in the middle of the rocks grew the tree.

Sita climbed into the tree to get a better view. She had climbed the tree many times and it took her only a few seconds to reach the higher branches. She put her hand to her eyes to shield them from the rain, and gazed upstream.

There was water everywhere. The world had become one vast river. Even the trees on the forested side of the river looked as though they had grown from the water, like mangroves. The sky was banked with massive, moisture-laden clouds. Thunder rolled down from the hills and the river seemed to take it up with a hollow booming sound.

Something was floating down with the current, something big and bloated. It was closer now, and Sita could make out the bulky object—a drowned buffalo, being carried rapidly downstream.

So the water had already inundated the villages further upstream. Or perhaps the buffalo had been grazing too close to the rising river.

Sita's worst fears were confirmed when, a little later, she saw planks of wood, small trees and bushes, and then a wooden bedstead, floating past the island.

How long would it take for the river to reach her own small hut?

As she climbed down from the tree, it began to rain more heavily. She ran indoors, shooing the hens before her. They flew into the hut and huddled under Grandmother's cot. Sita thought it would be best to keep them together now. And having them with her took away some of the loneliness.

There were three hens and a cock bird. The river did not bother them. They were interested only in food, and Sita kept them happy by throwing them a handful of onion skins.

She would have liked to close the door and shut out the swish of the rain and the boom of the river, but then she would have no way of knowing how fast the water rose.

She took Mumta in her arms, and began praying for the rain to stop and the river to fall. She prayed to the god Indra, and, just in case he was busy elsewhere, she prayed to other gods too. She prayed for the safety of her grandparents and for her own safety. She put herself last but only with great difficulty.

She would have to make herself a meal. So she chopped up some onions, fried them, then added turmeric and red chilli powder and stirred until she had everything sizzling; then she added a tumbler of water, some salt, and a cup of one of the cheaper lentils. She covered the pot and allowed the mixture to simmer.

Doing this took Sita about ten minutes. It would take at least half an hour for the dish to be ready.

When she looked outside, she saw pools of water amongst the rocks and near the tree. She couldn't tell if it was rainwater or overflow from the river.

She had an idea.

A big tin trunk stood in a corner of the room. It had belonged to Sita's mother. There was nothing in it except a cotton-filled quilt, for use during the cold weather. She would stuff the trunk with everything useful or valuable, and weigh it down so that it wouldn't be carried away, just in case the river came over the island.

Grandfather's hookah went into the trunk. Grandmother's walking stick went in too. So did a number of small tins containing the spices used in cooking—nutmeg, caraway seed, cinnamon, coriander and pepper—a bigger tin of flour and a tin of raw sugar. Even if Sita had to spend several hours in the tree, there would be something to eat when she came down again.

A clean white cotton shirt of Grandfather's, and Grandmother's only spare sari also went into the trunk. Never mind if they got stained with yellow curry powder! Never mind if they got to smell of salted fish, some of that went in too.

Sita was so busy packing the trunk that she paid no attention to the lick of cold water at her heels. She locked the trunk, placed the key high on the rock wall, and turned to give her attention to the lentils. It was only then that she discovered that she was walking about on a watery floor.

She stood still, horrified by what she saw. The water was oozing over the threshold, pushing its way into the room.

Sita was filled with panic. She forgot about her meal and everything else. Darting out of the hut, she ran splashing through ankle-deep water towards the safety of the peepul tree. If the tree hadn't been there, such a well-known landmark, she might have floundered into deep water, into the river.

She climbed swiftly into the strong arms of the tree, made herself secure on a familiar branch, and thrust the wet hair away from her eyes.

◆

She was glad she had hurried. The hut was now surrounded by water. Only the higher parts of the island could still be seen—a few rocks, the big rock on which the hut was built, a hillock on which some thorny bilberry bushes grew.

The hens hadn't bothered to leave the hut. They were probably perched on the cot now.

Would the river rise still higher? Sita had never seen it like this before. It swirled around her, stretching in all directions.

More drowned cattle came floating down. The most unusual things went by on the water—an aluminium kettle, a cane chair, a tin of tooth powder, an empty cigarette packet, a wooden slipper, a plastic doll…

A doll!

With a sinking feeling, Sita remembered Mumta.

Poor Mumta! She had been left behind in the hut. Sita, in her hurry, had forgotten her only companion.

Well, thought Sita, if I can be careless with someone I've

made, how can I expect the gods to notice me, alone in the middle of the river?

The waters were higher now, the island fast disappearing.

Something came floating out of the hut.

It was an empty kerosene tin, with one of the hens perched on top. The tin came bobbing along on the water, not far from the tree, and was then caught by the current and swept into the river. The hen still managed to keep its perch.

A little later, the water must have reached the cot because the remaining hens flew up to the rock ledge and sat huddled there in the small recess.

The water was rising rapidly now, and all that remained of the island was the big rock that supported the hut, the top of the hut itself and the peepul tree.

It was a tall tree with many branches and it seemed unlikely that the water could ever go right over it. But how long would Sita have to remain there? She climbed a little higher, and as she did so, a jet-black jungle crow settled in the upper branches, and Sita saw that there was a nest in them—a crow's nest, an untidy platform of twigs wedged in the fork of a branch.

In the nest were four blue-green, speckled eggs. The crow sat on them and cawed disconsolately. But though the crow was miserable, its presence brought some cheer to Sita. At least she was not alone. Better to have a crow for company than no one at all.

Other things came floating out of the hut—a large pumpkin; a red turban belonging to Grandfather, unwinding in the water like a long snake; and then—Mumta!

The doll, being filled with straw and wood shavings, moved quite swiftly on the water and passed close to the peepul tree. Sita saw it and wanted to call out, to urge her friend to make for the tree, but she knew that Mumta could not swim—the doll could only float, travel with the river, and perhaps be washed ashore many miles downstream.

The tree shook in the wind and the rain. The crow cawed and flew up, circled the tree a few times and returned to the nest. Sita clung to her branch.

The tree trembled throughout its tall frame. To Sita it felt like an earthquake tremor; she felt the shudder of the tree in her own bones.

The river swirled all around her now. It was almost up to the roof of the hut. Soon the mud walls would crumble and vanish. Except for the big rock and some trees far, far away, there was only water to be seen.

For a moment or two Sita glimpsed a boat with several people in it moving sluggishly away from the ruins of a flooded village, and she thought she saw someone pointing towards her, but the river swept them on and the boat was lost to view.

The river was very angry; it was like a wild beast, a dragon on the rampage, thundering down from the hills and sweeping across the plain, bringing with it dead animals, uprooted trees, household goods and huge fish choked to death by the swirling mud.

The tall old peepul tree groaned. Its long, winding roots clung tenaciously to the earth from which the tree had sprung many, many years ago. But the earth was softening, the stones were being washed away. The roots of the tree were rapidly losing their hold.

The crow must have known that something was wrong, because it kept flying up and circling the tree, reluctant to settle in it and reluctant to fly away. As long as the nest was there, the crow would remain, flapping about and cawing in alarm.

Sita's wet cotton dress clung to her thin body. The rain ran down from her long black hair. It poured from every leaf of the tree. The crow, too, was drenched and groggy.

The tree groaned and moved again. It had seen many monsoons. Once before, it had stood firm while the river had swirled around its massive trunk. But it had been young then.

Now, old in years and tired of standing still, the tree was ready to join the river.

With a flurry of its beautiful leaves, and a surge of mud from below, the tree left its place in the earth, and tilting, moved slowly forward, turning a little from side to side, dragging its roots along the ground. To Sita, it seemed as though the river was rising to meet the sky. Then the tree moved into the main current of the river, and went a little faster, swinging Sita from side to side. Her feet were in the water but she clung tenaciously to her branch.

◆

The branches swayed, but Sita did not lose her grip. The water was very close now. Sita was frightened. She could not see the extent of the flood or the width of the river. She could only see the immediate danger—the water surrounding the tree.

The crow kept flying around the tree. The bird was in a terrible rage. The nest was still in the branches, but not for long... The tree lurched and twisted slightly to one side, and the nest fell into the water. Sita saw the eggs go one by one.

The crow swooped low over the water, but there was nothing it could do. In a few moments, the nest had disappeared.

The bird followed the tree for about fifty yards, as though hoping that something still remained in the tree. Then, flapping its wings, it rose high into the air and flew across the river until it was out of sight.

Sita was alone once more. But there was no time for feeling lonely. Everything was in motion—up and down and sideways and forwards. 'Any moment,' thought Sita, 'the tree will turn right over and I'll be in the water!'

She saw a turtle swimming past—a great river turtle, the kind that feeds on decaying flesh. Sita turned her face away. In the distance, she saw a flooded village and people in flat-bottomed boats but they were very far away.

Because of its great size, the tree did not move very swiftly on the river. Sometimes, when it passed into shallow water, it stopped, its roots catching in the rocks; but not for long—the river's momentum soon swept it on.

At one place, where there was a bend in the river, the tree struck a sandbank and was still.

Sita felt very tired. Her arms were aching and she was no longer upright. With the tree almost on its side, she had to cling tightly to her branch to avoid falling off. The grey weeping sky was like a great shifting dome.

She knew she could not remain much longer in that position. It might be better to try swimming to some distant rooftop or tree. Then she heard someone calling. Craning her neck to look upriver, she was able to make out a small boat coming directly towards her.

The boat approached the tree. There was a boy in the boat who held on to one of the branches to steady himself, giving his free hand to Sita.

She grasped it, and slipped into the boat beside him.

The boy placed his bare foot against the tree trunk and pushed away.

The little boat moved swiftly down the river. The big tree was left far behind. Sita would never see it again.

◆

She lay stretched out in the boat, too frightened to talk. The boy looked at her, but he did not say anything, he did not even smile. He lay on his two small oars, stroking smoothly, rhythmically, trying to keep from going into the middle of the river. He wasn't strong enough to get the boat right out of the swift current, but he kept trying.

A small boat on a big river—a river that had no boundaries but which reached across the plains in all directions. The boat moved swiftly on the wild waters, and Sita's home was left far behind.

The boy wore only a loincloth. A sheathed knife was knotted into his waistband. He was a slim, wiry boy, with a hard flat belly; he had high cheekbones, strong white teeth. He was a little darker than Sita.

'You live on the island,' he said at last, resting on his oars and allowing the boat to drift a little, for he had reached a broader, more placid stretch of the river. 'I have seen you sometimes. But where are the others?'

'My grandmother was sick,' said Sita, 'so Grandfather took her to the hospital in Shahganj.'

'When did they leave?'

'Early this morning.'

Only that morning—and yet it seemed to Sita as though it had been many mornings ago.

'Where have you come from?' she asked. She had never seen the boy before.

'I come from...' he hesitated, '...near the foothills. I was in my boat, trying to get across the river with the news that one of the villages was badly flooded, but the current was too strong. I was swept down past your island. We cannot fight the river, we must go wherever it takes us.'

'You must be tired. Give me the oars.'

'No. There is not much to do now, except keep the boat steady.'

He brought in one oar, and with his free hand he felt under the seat where there was a small basket. He produced two mangoes, and gave one to Sita.

They bit deep into the ripe fleshy mangoes, using their teeth to tear the skin away. The sweet juice trickled down their chins. The flavour of the fruit was heavenly—truly this was the nectar of the gods! Sita hadn't tasted a mango for over a year. For a few moments she forgot about the flood—all that mattered was the mango!

The boat drifted, but not so swiftly now, for as they went further away across the plains, the river lost much of its tremendous force.

'My name is Krishan,' said the boy. 'My father has many cows and buffaloes, but several have been lost in the flood.'

'I suppose you go to school,' said Sita.

'Yes, I am supposed to go to school. There is one not far from our village. Do you have to go to school?'

'No—there is too much work at home.'

It was no use wishing she was at home—home wouldn't be there any more—but she wished, at that moment, that she had another mango.

Towards evening, the river changed colour. The sun, low in the sky, emerged from behind the clouds, and the river changed slowly from grey to gold, from gold to a deep orange, and then, as the sun went down, all these colours were drowned in the river, and the river took on the colour of the night.

The moon was almost at the full and Sita could see across the river, to where the trees grew on its banks.

'I will try to reach the trees,' said the boy, Krishan. 'We do not want to spend the night on the water, do we?'

And so he pulled for the trees. After ten minutes of strenuous rowing, he reached a turn in the river and was able to escape the pull of the main current.

Soon they were in a forest, rowing between tall evergreens.

◆

They moved slowly now, paddling between the trees, and the moon lighted their way, making a crooked silver path over the water.

'We will tie the boat to one of these trees,' said Krishan. 'Then we can rest. Tomorrow we will have to find our way out of the forest.'

He produced a length of rope from the bottom of the boat, tied one end to the boat's stern and threw the other end over a stout branch which hung only a few feet above the water. The boat came to rest against the trunk of the tree.

It was a tall, sturdy Toon tree—the Indian mahogany—and it was quite safe, for there was no rush of water here; besides, the trees grew close together, making the earth firm and unyielding.

But the denizens of the forest were on the move. The animals had been flooded out of their holes, caves and lairs, and were looking for shelter and dry ground.

Sita and Krishan had barely finished tying the boat to the tree when they saw a huge python gliding over the water towards them. Sita was afraid that it might try to get into the boat; but it went past them, its head above water, its great awesome length trailing behind, until it was lost in the shadows.

Krishan had more mangoes in the basket, and he and Sita sucked hungrily on them while they sat in the boat.

A big sambur stag came thrashing through the water. He did not have to swim; he was so tall that his head and shoulders remained well above the water. His antlers were big and beautiful.

'There will be other animals,' said Sita. 'Should we climb into the tree?'

'We are quite safe in the boat,' said Krishan. 'The animals are interested only in reaching dry land. They will not even hunt each other. Tonight, the deer is safe from the panther and the tiger. So lie down and sleep, and I will keep watch.'

Sita stretched herself out in the boat and closed her eyes, and the sound of the water lapping against the sides of the boat soon lulled her to sleep. She woke once, when a strange bird called overhead. She raised herself on one elbow, but Krishan was awake, sitting in the prow, and he smiled reassuringly at her. He looked blue in the moonlight, the colour of the young god Krishna, and for a few moments Sita was confused and wondered if the boy was indeed Krishna; but when she thought about it, she decided that it wasn't possible. He was just a village boy and she had seen hundreds like him—well, not exactly like him; he was different, in a way she couldn't explain to herself…

And when she slept again, she dreamt that the boy and Krishna were one, and that she was sitting beside him on a great white bird which flew over mountains, over the snow peaks of the Himalayas, into the cloud-land of the gods. There was a great rumbling sound, as though the gods were angry about the whole thing, and she woke up to this terrible sound and looked about her, and there in the moonlit glade, up to his belly in water, stood a young elephant, his trunk raised as he trumpeted his predicament to the forest—for he was a young elephant, and he was lost, and he was looking for his mother.

He trumpeted again, and then lowered his head and listened. And presently, from far away, came the shrill trumpeting of another elephant. It must have been the young one's mother, because he gave several excited trumpet calls, and then went stamping and churning through the flood water towards a gap in the trees. The boat rocked in the waves made by his passing.

'It's all right now,' said Krishan. 'You can go to sleep again.'

'I don't think I will sleep now,' said Sita.

'Then I will play my flute for you,' said the boy, 'and the time will pass more quickly.'

From the bottom of the boat he took a flute, and putting it to his lips, he began to play. The sweetest music that Sita had ever heard came pouring from the little flute, and it seemed to fill the forest with its beautiful sound. And the music carried her away again, into the land of dreams, and they were riding on the bird once more, Sita and the blue god, and they were passing through clouds and mist, until suddenly the sun shot out through the clouds. And at the same moment, Sita opened her eyes and saw the sun streaming through the branches of the Toon tree, its bright green leaves making a dark pattern against the blinding blue of the sky.

Sita sat up with a start, rocking the boat. There were hardly any clouds left. The trees were drenched with sunshine.

The boy Krishan was fast asleep in the bottom of the boat. His flute lay in the palm of his half-open hand. The sun came slanting across his bare brown legs. A leaf had fallen on his upturned face, but it had not woken him, it lay on his cheek as though it had grown there.

Sita did not move again. She did not want to wake the boy. It didn't look as though the water had gone down, but it hadn't risen, and that meant the flood had spent itself.

The warmth of the sun, as it crept up Krishan's body, woke him at last. He yawned, stretched his limbs, and sat up beside Sita.

'I'm hungry,' he said with a smile.

'So am I,' said Sita.

'The last mangoes,' he said, and emptied the basket of its last two mangoes.

After they had finished the fruit, they sucked the big seeds until these were quite dry. The discarded seeds floated well on the water. Sita had always preferred them to paper boats.

'We had better move on,' said Krishan.

He rowed the boat through the trees, and then for about an hour they were passing through the flooded forest, under the dripping branches of rain-washed trees. Sometimes they had to use the oars to push away vines and creepers. Sometimes drowned bushes hampered them. But they were out of the forest before noon.

Now the water was not very deep and they were gliding over flooded fields. In the distance, they saw a village. It was on high ground. In the old days, people had built their villages on hilltops, which gave them a better defence against bandits and invading armies. This was an old village, and though its inhabitants had long ago exchanged their swords for pruning forks, the hill on which it stood now protected it from the flood.

The people of the village—long-limbed, sturdy Jats—were generous, and gave the stranded children food and shelter. Sita was anxious to find her grandparents, and an old farmer who had business in Shahganj offered to take her there. She was hoping that Krishan would accompany her, but he said he would wait in the village, where he knew others would soon be arriving, his own people among them.

'You will be all right now,' said Krishan. 'Your grandfather will be anxious for you, so it is best that you go to him as soon as you can. And in two or three days, the water will go down and you will be able to return to the island.'

'Perhaps the island has gone forever,' said Sita.

As she climbed into the farmer's bullock cart, Krishan handed her his flute.

'Please keep it for me,' he said. 'I will come for it one day.' And when he saw her hesitate, he added, his eyes twinkling, 'It is a good flute!'

◆

It was slow going in the bullock cart. The road was awash, the wheels got stuck in the mud, and the farmer, his grown son and Sita had to keep getting down to heave and push in order to free the big wooden wheels. They were still in a foot or two of water. The bullocks were bespattered with mud, and Sita's legs were caked with it.

They were a day and a night in the bullock cart before they reached Shahganj; by that time, Sita, walking down the narrow bazaar of the busy market town, was hardly recognizable.

Grandfather did not recognize her. He was walking stiffly down the road, looking straight ahead of him, and would have walked right past the dusty, dishevelled girl if she had not charged straight at his thin, shaky legs and clasped him around the waist.

'Sita!' he cried, when he had recovered his wind and his balance. 'But how are you here? How did you get off the island? I was so worried—it has been very bad these last two days…'

'Is Grandmother all right?' asked Sita.

But even as she spoke, she knew that Grandmother was no longer with them. The dazed look in the old man's eyes told her as much. She wanted to cry, not for Grandmother, who could suffer no more, but for Grandfather, who looked so helpless and bewildered; she did not want him to be unhappy. She forced back her tears, took his gnarled and trembling hand, and led him down the crowded street. And she knew, then, that it would be on her shoulder that Grandfather would have to lean in the years to come.

They returned to the island after a few days, when the river was no longer in spate. There was more rain, but the worst was over. Grandfather still had two of the goats; it had not been necessary to sell more than one.

He could hardly believe his eyes when he saw that the tree had disappeared from the island—the tree that had seemed as permanent as the island, as much a part of his life as the river itself. He marvelled at Sita's escape. 'It was the tree that saved you,' he said.

'And the boy,' said Sita.

Yes, and the boy.

She thought about the boy, and wondered if she would ever see him again. But she did not think too much, because there was so much to do.

For three nights they slept under a crude shelter made out of jute bags. During the day, she helped Grandfather rebuild the mud hut. Once again, they used the big rock as a support.

The trunk which Sita had packed so carefully had not been swept off the island, but the water had got into it, and the food and clothing had been spoilt. But Grandfather's hookah had been saved, and, in the evenings, after their work was done and they had eaten the light meal which Sita prepared, he would smoke with a little of his old contentment, and tell Sita about other floods and storms which he had experienced as a boy.

Sita planted a mango seed in the same spot where the peepul tree had stood. It would be many years before it grew into a big tree, but Sita liked to imagine sitting in its branches one day, picking the mangoes straight from the tree, and feasting on them all day. Grandfather was more particular about making a vegetable garden and putting down peas, carrots, gram and mustard.

One day, when most of the hard work had been done and the new hut was almost ready, Sita took the flute which had been given to her by the boy, and walked down to the water's edge and tried to play it. But all she could produce were a few broken notes, and even the goats paid no attention to her music.

Sometimes, Sita thought she saw a boat coming down the river and she would run to meet it; but usually there was no boat, or if there was, it belonged to a stranger or to another fisherman. And so she stopped looking out for boats. Sometimes she thought she heard the music of a flute, but it seemed very distant and she could never tell where the music came from.

Slowly, the rains came to an end. The flood waters had receded, and in the villages people were beginning to till the land again and sow crops for the winter months. There were cattle fairs and wrestling matches. The days were warm and sultry. The water in the river was no longer muddy, and one evening Grandfather brought home a huge Mahseer fish and Sita made it into a delicious curry.

◆

Grandfather sat outside the hut, smoking his hookah. Sita was at the far end of the island, spreading clothes on the rocks to dry. One of the goats had followed her. It was the friendlier of the two, and often followed Sita about the island. She had made it a necklace of coloured beads.

She sat down on a smooth rock, and, as she did so, she noticed a small bright object in the sand near her feet. She stooped and picked it up. It was a little wooden toy—a coloured peacock—that must have come down on the river and been swept ashore on the island. Some of the paint had rubbed off, but for Sita, who had no toys, it was a great find. Perhaps it would speak to her, as Mumta had spoken to her.

As she held the toy peacock in the palm of her hand, she thought she heard the flute music again, but she did not look up. She had heard it before, and she was sure that it was all in her mind.

But this time the music sounded nearer, much nearer. There

was a soft footfall in the sand. And, looking up, she saw the boy, Krishan, standing over her.

'I thought you would never come,' said Sita.

'I had to wait until the rains were over. Now that I am free, I will come more often. Did you keep my flute?'

'Yes, but I cannot play it properly. Sometimes it plays by itself, I think, but it will not play for me!'

'I will teach you to play it,' said Krishan.

He sat down beside her, and they cooled their feet in the water, which was clear now, reflecting the blue of the sky. You could see the sand and the pebbles of the riverbed.

'Sometimes the river is angry, and sometimes it is kind,' said Sita.

'We are part of the river,' said the boy. 'We cannot live without it.'

It was a good river, deep and strong, beginning in the mountains and ending in the sea. Along its banks, for hundreds of miles, lived millions of people, and Sita was only one small girl among them, and no one had ever heard of her, no one knew her—except for the old man, the boy and the river.

CHACHI'S FUNERAL

Chachi died at 6 p.m. on Wednesday, 5 April, and came to life again exactly twenty minutes later. This is how it happened.

Chachi was, as a rule, a fairly tolerant, easy-going person, who waddled about the house without paying much attention to the swarms of small sons, daughters, nephews and nieces who poured in and out of the rooms. But she had taken a particular aversion to her ten-year-old nephew, Sunil. She was a simple woman and could not understand Sunil. He was a little brighter than her own sons, more sensitive, and inclined to resent a scolding or a cuff across the head. He was better-looking than her own children. All this, in addition to the fact that she resented having to cook for the boy while both his parents went out at office jobs, led her to grumble at him a little more than was really necessary.

Sunil sensed his aunt's jealousy and fanned its flames. He was a mischievous boy, and did little things to annoy her, like bursting paper-bags behind her while she dozed, or commenting on the width of her pyjamas when they were hung out to dry. On the evening of 5 April, he had been in particularly high spirits, and feeling hungry, entered the kitchen with the intention of helping himself to some honey. But the honey was on the top shelf, and Sunil wasn't quite tall enough to grasp the bottle. He got his fingers to it but as he tilted it towards him, it fell to the ground with a crash.

Chachi reached the scene of the accident before Sunil could slip away. Removing her slipper, she dealt him three or four furious blows across the head and shoulders. This done, she sat down on the floor and burst into tears.

Had the beating come from someone else, Sunil might have cried; but his pride was hurt, and instead of weeping, he muttered something under his breath and stormed out of the room.

Climbing the steps to the roof, he went to his secret hiding place, a small hole in the wall of the unused barsati, where he kept his marbles, kite-string, tops, and a clasp-knife. Opening the knife, he plunged it thrice into the soft wood of the window frame.

'I'll kill her!' he whispered fiercely, 'I'll kill her, I'll kill her!'

'Who are you going to kill, Sunil?'

It was his cousin Madhu, a dark slim girl of twelve, who aided and abetted him in most of his exploits. Sunil's chachi was her 'mammi'. It was a very big family.

'Chachi,' said Sunil. 'She hates me, I know. Well, I hate her too. This time I'll kill her.'

'How are you going to do it?'

'I'll stab with this.' He showed her the knife.

'Three times, in the heart.'

'But you'll be caught. The C.I.D. are very clever. Do you want to go to jail?'

'Won't they hang me?'

'They don't hang small boys. They send them to boarding schools.'

'I don't want to go to a boarding-school.'

'Then better not kill your Chachi. At least not this way. I'll show you how.'

Madhu produced pencil and paper, went down on her hands and knees, and screwing up her face in sharp concentration, made a rough drawing of Chachi. Then, with a red crayon, she sketched in a big heart in the region of Chachi's stomach.

'Now,' she said, 'stab her to death!'

Sunil's eyes shone with excitement. Here was a great new game. You could always depend on Madhu for something original. He held the drawing against the woodwork, and plunged his knife three times into Chachi's pastel breast.

'You have killed her,' said Madhu.

'Is that all?'

'Well, if you like, we can cremate her.'

'All right.'

She took the torn paper, crumpled it up, produced a box of matches from Sunil's hiding place, lit a match, and set fire to the paper. In a few minutes all that remained of Chachi were a few ashes.

'Poor Chachi,' said Madhu.

'Perhaps we shouldn't have done it,' said Sunil beginning to feel sorry.

'I know, we'll put her ashes in the river!'

'What river?'

'Oh, the drain will do.'

Madhu gathered the ashes together, and leant over the balcony of the roof. She threw out her arms, and the ashes drifted downwards.

Some of them settled on the pomegranate tree, a few reached the drain and were carried away by a sudden rush of kitchen water. She turned to face Sunil.

Big tears were rolling down Sunil's cheeks.

'What are you crying for?' asked Madhu.

'Chachi. I didn't hate her so much.'

'Then why did you want to kill her?'

'Oh, that was different.'

'Come on, then, let's go down. I have to do my homework.' As they came down the steps from the roof, Chachi emerged from the kitchen.

'Oh Chachi!' shouted Sunil. He rushed to her and tried to get his arms around her ample waist.

'Now what's up?' grumbled Chachi. 'What is it this time?' 'Nothing, Chachi. I love you so much. Please don't leave us.' A look of suspicion crossed Chachi's face. She frowned down at the boy. But she was reassured by the look of genuine affection that she saw in his eyes.

'Perhaps he *does* care for me, after all,' she thought and patting him gently on the head, she took him by the hand and led him back to the kitchen.

MISS BUN AND OTHERS

1 March 1975

Beer in the sun. High in the spruce tree the barbet calls, heralding summer. A few puffy clouds drift lazily over the mountains. Is this the great escape?

I could sit here all day soaking up beer and sunshine, but at some time during the day I must wipe the dust from my typewriter and produce something readable. There's only eight hundred rupees in the bank, book sales are falling off, and magazines are turning away from fiction.

Prem spoils me, giving me rice and kofta curry for lunch, which means that I sleep till four when Miss Bun arrives with patties and samosas.

Miss Bun is the baker's daughter.

Of course that's not her real name. Her real name is very long and beautiful, but I won't give it here for obvious reasons and also because her brother is big and ugly.

I am seeing Miss Bun after two months. She's been with relatives in Bareilly.

She sits at the foot of my bed, absolutely radiant. Her raven-black hair lies loose on her shoulders, her eyelashes have been trimmed and blackened and so have her eyes, with kajal. Her eyes, so large and innocent—and calculating!

There are pretty glass bangles on her wrists and she wears a pair of new slippers. Her kameez is new too—green silk, with gold embroidered sleeves.

'You must have a rich lover,' I remark, taking her hand and gently pulling her towards me. 'Who gave you all this finery?'

'You did. Don't you remember? Before I went away, you gave me a hundred rupees.'

'That was for the train and bus fares, I thought.'

'Oh, my uncle paid the fares. So I bought myself these things. Are they nice?'

'Very pretty. And so are you. If you were ten years older and I ten years younger, we'd make a good pair. But I'd have been broke long before this!'

She giggles and drops a paper bag full of samosas on the bedside table. I hate samosas and patties, but I keep ordering them because it gives Miss Bun a pretext for visiting me. It's all in the way of helping the bakery get by. When she goes, I give the lot to Bijju and Binya or whoever might be passing.

'You've been away a long time,' I complain. 'What if I'd got married while you were away?'

'Then you'd stop ordering samosas.'

'Or get them from that old man Bashir, who makes much better ones, and cheaper!'

She drops her head on my shoulder. Her hair is heavily scented with jasmine hair oil, and I nearly pass out. They should use it instead of anaesthesia.

'You smell very nice,' I lie. 'Do I get a kiss?'

She gives me a long kiss, as though to make up for her long absence. Her kisses always have a nice wholesome flavour, as you would expect from someone who lives in a bakery.

'That was an expensive kiss.'

'I want to buy some face cream.'

'You don't need face cream. Your complexion is perfect. It

must be the good quality flour you use in the bakery.'

'I don't put flour on my face. Anyway, I want the cream for my elder sister. She has pockmarks.'

I surrender and give her two fives, quickly putting away my wallet.

'And when will you pay for the samosas?'

'Next week.'

'I'll bring you something nice next week,' she says, pausing in the doorway.

'Well, thanks, I was getting tired of samosas.'

She was gone in a twinkling.

I'll say this for Miss Bun—she doesn't trouble to hide her intentions.

March 4

My policeman calls on me this morning. Ghanshyam, the constable attached to the Barlowganj outpost.

He is not very tall for a policeman, and he has a round, cheerful countenance, which is unusual in his profession. He looks smart in his uniform. Most constables prefer to hang around in their pyjamas most of the time.

Nothing alarming about Ghanshyam's visit. He comes to see me about once a week, and has been doing so ever since I spent a night in the police station last year.

It happened when I punched a Muzzaffarnagar businessman in the eye for bullying a rickshaw coolie. The fat slob very naturally lodged a complaint against me, and that same evening a sub-inspector called and asked me to accompany him to the thana. It was too late to arrange anything and in any case I had only been taken in for questioning, so I had to spend the night at the police post. The sub-inspector went home and left me in the charge of a constable. A wooden bench and a charpoy were the only items of furniture in my cell, if you could call it that. The charpoy was meant for the night-duty constable, but he very generously offered it to me.

'But where will you sleep?' I asked.

'Oh, I don't feel like sleeping. Usually I go to the night show at the Picture Palace, but I suppose I'll have to stay here because of you.'

He looked rather sulky. Obviously I'd ruined his plans for the night.

'You don't have to stay because of me,' I said. 'I won't tell the SHO. You go to the Picture Palace, I'll look after the thana.'

He brightened up considerably, but still looked a bit doubtful.

'You can trust me,' I said encouragingly. 'My grandfather was a private soldier who became a Buddhist.'

'Then I can trust you as far as your grandfather.' He was quite cheerful now, and sent for two cups of tea from the shop across the road. It came gratis, of course. A little later he left me, and I settled down on the cot and slept fitfully. The constable came back during the early hours and went to sleep on the bench. Next morning I was allowed to go home. The Muzzaffarnagar businessman had got into another fight and was lodged in the main thana. I did not hear about the matter again.

Ghanshyam, the constable, having struck up a friendship with me, was to visit me from time to time.

And here he is today, boots shining, teeth gleaming, cheeks almost glowing, far too charming a person to be a policeman.

'Hello, Ghanshyam bhai,' I welcome him. 'Sit down and have some tea.'

'No, I can't stop for long,' he says, but sits down beside me on the verandah steps. 'Can you do me a favour?'

'Sure. What is it?'

'I'm fed up with Barlowganj. I want to get a transfer.'

'And how can I help you? I don't know any netas or bigwigs.'

'No, but our SP will be here next week and he can have me transferred. Will you speak to him?'

'But why should he listen to me?'

'Well, you see, he has a weakness…'

'We all have our weaknesses. Does your SP have a weakness similar to mine? Do we proceed to blackmail him?'

'Yes. You see, he writes poetry. And you are a *kavi*, a poet, aren't you?'

'At times,' I concede. 'And I have to admit it's a weakness, especially as no one cares to read my poetry.'

'No one reads the SP's poetry, either. Although we have to listen to it sometimes. When he has finished reading out one of his poems, we salute and say "Shabash!"'

'A captive audience. I wish I had one.'

Ignoring my sarcasm, Ghanshyam continues: 'The trouble is, he can't get anyone to publish his poems. This makes him bad tempered and unsympathetic to applications for transfer. Can you help?'

'I am not a publisher. I can only salute like the rest of you.'

'But you know publishers, don't you? If you can get some of his poems published, he'd be very grateful. To you. To me. To both of us!'

'You really are an optimist.'

'Just one or two poems. You see, I've already told him about you. How you spent all night in the lock-up writing verses. He thinks you are a famous writer. He's depending on me now. If his poems get published he will give me a transfer. I'm sick of Barlowganj!' He gives me a hug and pinches me on the cheek.

Before he can go any further, I say: 'Well, I'll do my best'—I am thinking of a little magazine published in Bhopal where most of my rejects find a home. 'For your sake, I'll try. But first I must see the poems.'

'You shall even see the SP,' he promises. 'I'll bring him here next week. You can give him a cup of tea.'

He gets up, gives me a smart salute and goes up the path with a spring in his step. The sort of man who knows how to get his transfers and promotions in a perfectly honest manner.

March 7

It gets warmer day by day.

This morning I decided to sunbathe—quite modestly, of course. Retaining my old khaki shorts but removing all other clothing, I stretched out on a mattress in the garden. Almost immediately I was disturbed by the baker (Miss Bun's father for a change), who presented me with two loaves of bread and half a dozen chocolate pastries, ordered the previous day. Then Prem's small son, Raki, turned up, demanding a pastry, and I gave him two. He insisted on joining me on the mattress, where he proceeded to drop crumbs in my hair and on my chest. 'Good morning, Mr Bond!' came the dulcet tones of Mrs Biggs, leaning over the gate. Forgetting that she was short-sighted, I jumped to my feet, and at the same time my shorts slipped down over my knees. As I grabbed for them, Mrs Biggs's effusiveness reached greater heights. 'Why, what a lovely *agapanthus* you've got!' she exclaimed, referring no doubt to the solitary lily in the garden. I must confess I blushed. Then, recovering myself, I returned her greeting, remarking on the freshness of the morning.

Mrs Biggs, at eighty, was a little deaf as well, and replied, 'I'm very well, thank you, Mr Bond. Is that a child you're carrying?'

'Yes, Prem's small son.'

'Prem is your son? I didn't know you had a family.' At this point Raki decided to pluck the spectacles off Mrs Biggs's nose, and after I had recovered them for her, she beat a hasty retreat. Later, Rev. Mr Biggs came over to borrow a book.

'Just light reading,' he said. 'I can't concentrate for long periods.'

He has become extremely absent-minded and forgetful; one of the drawbacks of living to an advanced age. During a funeral last year at which he took the funeral service, he read out the service for Burial at Sea. It was raining heavily at the time, and no one seemed to notice.

Now he has borrowed two of my Ross Macdonalds—the same two he read last month. I refrained from pointing this out. If he has forgotten the books already, it won't matter if he reads them again.

Having spent the better part of his seventy-odd years in India, Rev. Biggs has a lot of stories to tell, his favourite being the one about the crocodile he shot in Orissa when he was a young man. He'd pitched his tent on the banks of a river and gone to sleep on a camp cot. During the night he felt his cot moving, and before he could gather his wits, the cot had moved swiftly through the opening of the tent and was rapidly making its way down to the river. Mr Biggs leapt for dry land while the cot, firmly wedged on the back of the crocodile, disappeared into the darkness.

Crocodiles, it seems, often bury themselves in the mud when they go to sleep, and Mr Biggs had pitched his tent and made his bed on top of a sleeping crocodile. Waking in the night, it had made for the nearest water.

Mr Biggs shot it the following morning—or so he would have us believe—the crocodile having reappeared on the river bank with the cot still attached to its back.

Now having told me this story for the umpteenth time, Biggs said he really must be going, and returning to the bookshelf, extracted Gibbons' *Decline and Fall of the Roman Empire,* having forgotten the Ross Macdonalds on a side table.

'I must do some serious reading,' he said. 'These modern novels are so violent.'

'Lots of violence in *Decline and Fall,*' I remarked.

'Ah, but it's history, isn't it? Well, I must go now, Mr Macdonald. Mustn't waste your time.'

As he stepped outside, he collided with Miss Bun, who dropped samosas all over the verandah steps.

'Oh, dear, I'm so sorry,' he apologized, and started picking up the samosas despite my attempts to prevent him from doing so. He then took the paper bag from Miss Bun and replaced the samosas.

'And who is this little girl?' he said benignly, patting Miss Bun on the head. 'One of your nieces?'

'That's right, sir. My favourite niece.'

'Well, I must not keep you. Service as usual, on Sunday.'

'Right, Mr Biggs.'

I have never been to a local church service, but why disillusion Rev. Biggs? I shall defend everyone's right to go to a place of worship provided they allow me the freedom to stay away.

Miss Bun was staring after Rev. Biggs as he crossed the road. Her mouth was slightly agape. 'What's the matter?' I asked.

'He's taken all the samosas!'

When I kiss Miss Bun, she bites my lip and draws blood.

'What was that for?' I complain.

'Just to make you angry.'

'But I don't like getting angry.'

'That's why.'

I get angry just to please her, and we take a tumble on the carpet.

March 11

Does anyone here make money? Apart from the traders, of course, who tuck it all away…

A young man turned up yesterday, selling geraniums. He had a bag full of geraniums—cuttings and whole plants.

'All colours,' he told me confidently. 'Only one rupee a cutting.'

'I can buy them much cheaper at the government nursery.'

'But you would have to walk there, sir—six miles! I have brought these to your very doorstep. I will plant them for you in your empty ghee tins at no extra cost!'

'That's all right, you can give me a few. But what makes you sell geraniums?'

'I have nothing to eat, sir. I haven't eaten for two days.'

He must have sold all his plants that day, because in the evening I saw him at the country liquor shop, tippling away—and all on an empty stomach, I presume!

March 12

Mrs Biggs tells me that someone slipped into her garden yesterday morning while she was out, and removed all her geraniums!

'The most honest of people won't hesitate to steal flowers—or books,' I remark carelessly. 'Never mind, Mrs Biggs, you can have some of my geraniums. I bought them yesterday.'

'That's extremely kind of you, Mr Bond. And you've only just put them down, I can tell,' she says, spotting the cuttings in the Dalda tins. 'No, I couldn't deprive you—'

'I'll get you some,' I offer, and generously surrender half the geraniums, vowing that if ever I come across that young man again, I'll get him to recover all the plants he sold elsewhere.

March 19

Vinod, now selling newspapers, arrives as I am pouring myself a beer under the cherry tree. It's a warm day and I can see he is thirsty.

'Can I have a drink of water?' he asks.

'Would you like some beer'?'

'Yes, *sir!*'

As I have an extra bottle, I pour him a glass and he squats on the grass near the old wall and brings me up to date on the local gossip. There are about fifty papers in his shoulder hag, yet to be delivered.

'You may feel drowsy after some time,' I warn. 'Don't leave your papers in the wrong houses.'

'Nothing to worry about,' he says, emptying the glass and gazing fondly at the bottle sparkling in the spring sunshine.

'Have some more,' I tell him, and go indoors to see what Prem is making for lunch. (Stuffed gourds, fried brinjal slices and pilaf. Prem is in a good mood, preparing my favourite dishes. When I upset him, he gives me string beans.) Returning to the garden, I find Vinod well into his second glass of beer. Half of Barlowganj and all of Jharipani (the next village) are snarling and cursing, waiting for their newspapers.

'Your customers must be getting impatient,' I remark. 'Surely they want to know the result of the cricket test.' 'Oh, they heard it on the radio. This is the morning edition. I can deliver it in the evening.'

I go indoors and have my lunch with little Raki, and ask

Prem to give Vinod something to eat. When I come outside again, he is stretched out under the cherry tree, burping contentedly.

'Thank you for the lunch,' he says, and closes his eyes and goes to sleep.

He's gone by evening but his bag of papers rests against my front door.

'He's left his papers behind,' I remark to Prem.

'Oh, he'll deliver them tomorrow, along with tomorrow's paper. He'll say the mail bus was late due to a landslide.'

In the evening I walk through the old bazaar and linger in front of a Tibetan shop, gazing at the brassware, coloured stones, amulets, masks. I am about to pass on, when I catch a glimpse of the girl who looks after the shop. Two soft brown eyes in a round jade-smooth face. A hesitant smile.

I step inside. I have never cared much for Tibetan handicrafts, but beautiful brown eyes are different.

'Can I look around? I want to buy a present for a friend.'

I look around. She helps me by displaying bangles, necklaces, rings—all on the assumption that my friend is a young lady.

I choose the more frightening of two devil masks, and promise to come again for the pair to it.

On the way home I meet Miss Bun.

'When shall I come?' she asks, pirouetting on the road.

'Next year.'

'Next year!' Her pretty mouth falls open.

'That's right,' I say. 'You've just lost the election.'

March 31

Miss Bun hasn't been for several days. This morning I find her washing clothes at the public tap. She gives me a quick smile as I pass.

'It's nice to see you hard at work,' I remark.

She looks quickly left and right, then says, 'It's punishment, because I bought new bangles with the money you gave me.'

I hurry on down the road.

During the afternoon siesta I am roused by someone knocking on the door. A slim boy with thick hair and bushy eyebrows is standing there. I don't know him, but his eyes remind me of someone.

He tells me he is Miss Bun's older brother. At a guess, he would be only a year or two older than her.

'Come in,' I say. It's best to be friendly! What could he possibly want?

He produces a bag of samosas and puts them down on my bedside table.

'My sister cannot come this week. I will bring you samosas instead. Is that all right?'

'Oh, sure. Sit down, sit down. So you're Master Bun. It's nice to know you.'

He sits down on the edge of the bed and studies the picture on the wall—a print of Kurosawa's *Wave*.

'Shall I pay you now for the samosas?' I ask.

'No, no, whenever you like.'

'And do you go to school or college?'

'No, I help my father in the bakery. Are you ill, sir?'

'No. What makes you think so?'

'Because you were lying down.'

'Well, I like lying down. It's. better than standing up. And I do get a headache if I read or write for too long.'

He offers to give me a head massage, and I submit to his ministrations for about five minutes. The headache is now much worse, but I pay for both massage and samosas and tell him he can come again—preferably next year.

My next visitor is Constable Ghanshyam Singh, who tells me that the SP has extracted confessions from a couple of thieves simply by making them stand for hours and listen to him reciting his poetry. I know our police have a reputation for torturing suspects, but I think this is carrying things a bit too far.

'And what about your transfer?' I ask.

'As soon as those poems are published in the *Weekly*.'

'I'll do my best,' I promise.

(They appeared in the Bhopal *Weekly*. And a year later, when I was editing *Imprint*, I was able to publish one of the SP's poems. He has always maintained that if I'd published more of them, the magazine would never have folded.)

A note on Miss Bun
Little Miss Bun is fond of bed,
But she keeps a cash box in her head.

April 8

Rev. Biggs at the door, book in hand.

'I won't take up your time, Mr Bond. But I thought it was time I returned your butterfly book.'

'My butterfly book?'

'Yes, thank you very much. I enjoyed it a great deal.'

Mr Biggs hands me the book on butterflies, a handsomely illustrated volume. It isn't my book, but if Mr Biggs insists on giving me someone else's book, who am I to quibble? He'd never find the right owner, anyway.

'By the way, have you seen Mrs Biggs?' he asks.

'No, not this morning, sir.'

'She went off without telling me. She's always doing things like that. Very irritating.'

After he has gone, I glance at the fly leaf of the book. It says W. Biggs. So it's one of his own…

A little later Mrs Biggs comes by.

'Have you seen Will?' she asks.

'He was here about fifteen minutes ago. He was looking for you.'

'Oh, he knew I'd gone to the garden shed. How tiresome! I suppose he's wandered off somewhere.'

'Never mind, Mrs Biggs, he'll make his way home when he gets hungry. A good lunch will always bring a wanderer home. By the way, I've got his book on butterflies. Perhaps you'd return it to him for me? And he shouldn't lend it to just anyone, you know. It's a valuable book, you don't want to lose it.'

'I'm sure it was quite safe with you, Mr Bond.'

Books always are, of course. On principle, I never steal another man's books. I might take his geraniums or his old school tie, but I wouldn't deprive him of his books. Or the song or melody or dream he lives by. And here's a little lullaby for Raki:

Little one, don't be afraid of this big river.
Be safe in these warm arms for ever.
Grow tall, my child, be wise and strong.
But do not take from any man his song.
Little one, don't be afraid of this dark night.
Walk boldly as you see the truth and light.
Love well, my child, laugh all day long,
But do not take from any man his song.

April 16

Is there something about the air at this height that makes people light-headed, absent-minded? Ten years from now I will probably be as forgetful as Mr Biggs. I must climb the next mountain before I forget where it is.

Outline for a story:

Someone lives in a small hut near a spring, within sound of running water. He never leaves the place, except to walk into the town for books, post and supplies. 'Don't you ever get bored here?' I ask. 'Do you never wish to leave?' 'No,' he replies, and tells me of his experience in the desert, when for two days and two nights (the limit of human endurance in regard to thirst), he went without water. On the second night, half dead, lying in the open beneath the stars, he dreamt of just such a spring in the mountains, and it was as though it gave him spiritual sustenance. So later, when he was fully recovered, he went in search of the spring (which he was sure existed), and found it while hiking in the Himalayas. He knew that as long as he remained by the spring he would never feel unsafe; it was where his guardian spirit lived…

And so I feel safe near my own spring, my own mountain, for this is where my guardian spirit lives too.

April 16

Visited the Tibetan shop and bought a small brass vase encrusted with pretty stones.

I'd no intention of buying anything, but the girl smiled at me as I passed, and then I just had to go in; and once in, I couldn't just stand there, a fatuous grin on my face.

I had to buy something. And a vase is always a good thing to buy. If you don't like it, you can give it away.

If she smiles at me every time I pass, I shall probably build up a collection of vases.

She isn't a girl, really; she's probably about thirty. I suppose she has a husband who smuggles Chinese goods in from Nepal, while her children—'charity cases'—go to one of the posh public schools. But she's fresh and pretty, and then, of course, I don't have many young women smiling at me these days. I shall be forty-three next month.

April 17

Miss Bun still smiles at me, even though I frown at her when we pass.

This afternoon she brought me samosas and a rose.

'Where's your brother?' I asked gruffly. 'He has more to talk about.'

'He's busy in the bakery. See, I've brought you a rose.'

'How much did it cost?'

'Don't be silly. It's a present.'

'Thanks. I didn't know you grew roses.'

'I don't. It's from the school garden.'

'Well, thank you anyway. You actually stole something on my behalf!'

'Where shall I put it?'

I found my new vase, filled it with fresh water, placed the rose in it and set it down on my dressing table.

'It leaks,' remarked Miss Bun.

'My vase?' I was incredulous.

'See, the water's spreading all over your nice table.'

She was right, of course. Water from the bottom of the vase was running across the varnished wood of great-grandmother's old rosewood dressing table. The stain, I felt sure, would be permanent.

'But it's a new vase!' I protested.

'Someone must have cheated you. Why did you buy it

without looking properly?'

'Well, you see, I didn't buy it actually. Someone gave it to me as a present.'

I fumed inwardly, vowing never again to visit the brassware shop. Never trust a smiling woman! I prefer Miss Bun's scowl.

'Do you want the vase?' she asks.

'No. Take it away.'

She places the rose on my pillow, throws the water out of the window and drops the vase into her cloth shopping bag.

'What will you do with it?' I ask.

'I'll seal the leak with flour,' she says.

April 21

A clear fresh morning after a week of intermittent rain. And what a morning for birds! Three doves courting, a cuckoo calling, a bunch of minas squabbling, and a pair of king crows doing Swedish exercises.

I find myself doing exercises of an original nature, devised by Master Bun. These consist of various contortions of the limbs which, he says, are good for my sex drive.

'But I don't want a sex drive,' I tell him. 'I want something that will take my mind *off* sex.'

So he gives me another set of exercises which consist mostly of deep breathing.

'Try holding your breath for five minutes,' he suggests.

'I know of someone who committed suicide by doing just that.'

'Then hold it for two minutes.'

I take a deep breath and last only a minute.

'No good,' he says. 'You have to relax more.'

'Well, I am tired of trying to relax. It doesn't work this

way. What I need is a good meal.'

And Prem obliges by serving up my favourite kofta curry and rice. Satiated, I have no problem in relaxing for the rest of the afternoon.

April 28

Master Bun wears a troubled expression.

'It's about my sister,' he says.

'What about her?' I ask, fearing the worst.

'She has run away.'

'That's bad. On her own?'

'No… With a professor.'

'That should be all right. Professors are usually respectable people. Maths or English?'

'I don't know. He has a wife and children.'

'Then obviously he hasn't taken them along.'

'He has taken her to Roorkee. My sister is an innocent girl.'

'Well, there is a certain innocence about her,' I say, recalling Nobokov's *Lolita*. 'Maybe the professor wants to adopt her.'

'But she's a virgin.'

'Then she must be rescued! Why are you here, talking to me about it, when you should be rushing down to Roorkee?'

'That's why I've come. Can you lend me the bus fare?'

'Better still, I'll come with you. We must rescue the professor—sorry, I mean your sister!'

May 1

—*Roorkee, to Roorkee, to find a sweet girl,*
Home again, home again, oh, what a whirl!

We did everything except find Miss Bun. Our first evening in Roorkee, we roamed the bazaar and the canal banks; the second day we did the rounds of the university, the regimental barracks and the headquarters of the Boys' Brigade. We made inquiries from all the bakers in Roorkee (many of them known to Master Bun), but none of them had seen his sister. On the college campus we asked for the professor, but no one had heard of him either.

Finally, we bought platform tickets and sat down on a bench at the end of the railway platform and watched the arrival and departure of trains, and the people who got on and off; we saw no one who looked in the least like Miss Bun. Master Bun bought an astrological guide from the station bookstall and studied his sister's horoscope to see if that might help, but it didn't. At the same bookstall, hidden under a pile of pirated Harold Robbins novels, I found a book of mine that had been published ten years earlier. No one had bought it in all that time. I replaced it at the top of the pile. Never lose hope!

On the third day we returned to Barlowganj and found Miss Bun at home.

She had gone no further than Debra's Paltan Bazaar, it seemed, and had ditched the professor there, having first made him buy her three dress pieces, two pairs of sandals, a sandalwood hair brush, a bottle of scent, and a satchel for her school books.

May 5

And now it's Mr Biggs's turn to disappear.

'Have you seen our Will?' asks Mrs Biggs at my gate.

'Not this morning, Mrs Biggs.'

'I can't find him anywhere. At breakfast he said he was going out for a walk, but nobody knows where he went, and he isn't in the school compound, I've just inquired. He's been gone over three hours!'

'Don't worry, Mrs Biggs. He'll turn up. Someone on the hillside must have asked him in for a cup of tea, and he's sitting there talking about the crocodile he shot in Orissa.'

But at lunchtime, Mr Biggs hadn't returned; and that was alarming, because Mr Biggs had never been known to miss his favourite egg curry and pilaf.

We organized a search. Prem and I walked the length of the Barlowganj bazaar and even lodged an unofficial report with Constable Ghanshyam. No one had seen him in the bazaar. Several members of the school staff combed the hillside without picking up the scent.

Mid-afternoon, while giving my negative report to Mrs Biggs, I heard a loud thumping coming from the direction of her storeroom.

'What's all that noise downstairs?' I asked.

'Probably rats. I don't hear anything.'

I ran downstairs and opened the storeroom door, and there was Mr Biggs looking very dusty and very disgruntled. He wanted to know why the devil (the first time he'd taken the devil's name in vain) Mrs Biggs had shut him up for hours. He'd gone into the storeroom in search of an old walking stick, and Mrs Biggs, seeing the door open, had promptly bolted it, failing to hear her husband's cries for immediate release. But for Mr Bond's presence of mind, he averred, he might have been discovered years later, a mere skeleton!

The cook was still out hunting for him, so Mr Biggs had his egg curry cold. Still in a foul mood, he sat down and wrote a letter to his sister in Tunbridge Wells, asking her to send over a hearing aid for Mrs Biggs.

Constable Ghanshyam turned up in the evening to inform

me that Mr Biggs had last been seen at Rajpur in the foothills, in the company of several gypsies!

'Never mind,' I said. 'These old men get that way. One last fling, one last romantic escapade, one last tilt at the windmill. If you have a dream, Ghanshyam, don't let them take it away from you.'

He looked puzzled, but went on to tell me that he was being transferred to Bareilly jail, where they keep those who have been found guilty but of unsound mind. It's a reward, no doubt, for his services in getting the SP's poems published. These journal entries date back some twenty years. What happened to Miss Bun? Well, she finally opened a beauty parlour in New Delhi, but I still can't tell you where it is, or give you her name.

Two or three years later, Mrs Biggs was laid to rest near her old friends in the Mussoorie cemetery. Rev. Biggs was flown home to Tunbridge Wells and his sister gave him a solid tombstone, so that he wasn't tempted to get up and wander off somewhere, in search of crocodiles.

A lot can happen in twenty years, and unfortunately not all of it gets recorded. 'Little Raki' is today a married man!

www.ingramcontent.com/pod-product-compliance
Lightning Source LLC
Chambersburg PA
CBHW041753010726
47507CB00009B/383